HOLLIDAY'S GOLD

A MODERN RE-TELLING OF "GOLDILOCKS & THE THREE BEARS"

HOLLIDAY'S GOLD

A MODERN RE-TELLING OF "GOLDILOCKS & THE THREE BEARS"

Steeven R. Orr

Cover by Harold C. Jennett III

www.steevenorrelse.com

www.haroldjennett.wordpress.com

Big Beard Books
2014

www.bigbeardbooks.com

For K. My life, my love, my lobster.

This book was written to the music of:

Adam WarRock
www.adamwarrock.com

•

MC Frontalot
www.frontalot.com

•

Mikal kHill
www.mikalkhill.com

•

Kirby Krackle
www.kirbykracklemusic.com

•

Support Independent Art

AUTHOR'S FOREWORD

O kay, before I get into anything here, I want to thank you for taking a chance on this, my very first novel. It amounts to three years of my life and it feels good knowing that someone is reading it.

Next, if you want to go ahead and skip this introduction here, you go right on ahead. I won't blame you. I've jumped over many an introduction in my day, so you can do so without the feeling of guilt that may set in by doing such a thing.

Now that we have that out of the way, what follows is just a little something that briefly explains how this tale came to be.

See, once upon a time, I used to run a blog called *Steeven's Place*. It's no longer around so there's really no point in looking for it. I had created the blog to force myself to write. The way my brain works, or the way it's supposed to work, is that when I am faced with some sort of deadline, even if it is a self-imposed deadline, I will get the work done. So, if I have a place on-line where I'm expected to write and post something each week, then I'll get it done.

That was the idea, anyway, and for a while it was working just fine. Then, in July of 2011, I had begun to take this whole writing thing a bit more seriously. The problem was, at the very same time, I had hit a creative wall. I had the blog up there, a place that was supposed to give me a reason to write. Yet, I had nothing percolating in the old brain region. Thus, I had begun to feel a mite discouraged regarding this little scheme of mine in which I get into the writing game.

At the time I had been talking to a friend of mine, Harold Jennett (an amazing artist, I mean it. Seriously, Google his name, or just look at the cover. Yeah, that's Harold), and I was lamenting on the fact that when it came to creating daily or even weekly content for a blog, comic book artists had it easy. They can just make a list of characters they want to sketch and there you go. A sketch a day.

Boom.

Content.

I apologize to all the artists out there because I know it's really not that easy, but I was in a bad place at the time and had to lash out at something. And, as it was no longer in fashion to blame all your problems on the Communists, I set my sights on artists.

That, of course, was not meant to be taken seriously.

Anyway, Harold tells me that maybe I could just do the same thing as a sketch-a-day posting schedule, only with words. His idea was a simple one. He suggested that I just start writing a story and post what I've written each day at a hundred or so words at a time.

Well, it was a genius idea, and after getting over the fact that I didn't come up with it myself, I began to plan. It took me no more than two minutes before I hit another wall. I still didn't have any idea of what I was going to write about.

Then I thought of *Goldilocks and the Three Bears*. See, I had read it to my kids only just the week before, and I remember while reading it that I thought it would be a fun writing exercise to rewrite the story using my own take.

So I did just that. For the next four months I wrote my story in forty-seven parts. I had no idea where I was going with it day to day, I just wrote. In fact, it wasn't until I was maybe 50% of the way through before I had a real handle on where I was headed with the story and how to end it. It's called seat-of-your-pants writing, and I had a great big bunch of fun with it.

Once the tale was complete and posted, Harold urged me to publish it, but I felt the story wasn't done. To me it felt like a first draft, and a rather rough first draft at that. The next step then would be to revise it. Beef it up some. It was a great opportunity because as I said, I didn't really know where I was going until I was halfway in, and when you are serializing a story like that on-line, you can't really go back to previous installments and change them to fit in with the direction you had suddenly sprung upon. But now I could ... and so I did. That's what you have before you now.

Enjoy.

PROLOGUE

HE WOKE TO THE sound of his own coughing.

The cough – a dry, hacking bark – reverberated through his entire body. It took control over every muscle and sent a sharp stinging pain into each nerve. He'd been living with the cough for a number of years, and now he would die with it.

After a few moments, the coughing subsided. He opened his eyes to blinding sunlight that shone through the bank of windows behind his bed. He shaded his eyes with a hand and had to blink away the pain that the light brought as it bounced off of the snow on the other side of the glass.

He thought about going back to sleep, but he knew it wouldn't last. Besides, he'd be dead soon. He could sleep all he wanted then.

He sat up and looked around the room in which he would spend his remaining days. A strange amalgamation of rustic hunting lodge and sterile hospital, he imagined it to be the sort of place where doctors would spend their work hours tending to patients, and their off hours killing a few of God's creatures.

His wasn't the only bed in the room, though it *was* the only one currently occupied. This suited him just fine. He thought he might like to die without a lot of fuss and bother. Besides, if others were sharing the room with him, they'd likely be in the same state as him, and he didn't quite feel up spending his last few hours on Earth listening to others wail and moan in anguish. Just the thought of it made him sick. In total, there were twelve beds in the room, six on his side, six on the opposite. That would have been a lot of whining and crying were the place full. Sometimes you just had to count your blessings.

He thought about leaving. Just climbing out of bed, pulling on his boots, and finding some decent place to die. A saloon, for example. He'd always figured he'd die in a saloon. A winning hand of poker in one hand and a six shooter in the other. At least he could have one last shot of whiskey before the lights went out on him. The thought of whisky made him smile. They didn't allow him any whisky in this place. No whisky, no women, and absolutely no fun.

A nurse entered the room with fresh water. She looked cheerful and happy; the very embodiment of optimism and hope. He hated her for that reason alone.

"Good morning," she sang. "How are we feeling?"

"I won't be so bold as to speak for you, darlin', but I feel like crap," he said.

The nurse put the water on the little table to the right of his bed and checked his bedding. "You just tell me what you need," she said, her face twisting into a smile that he thought made her look like a witless moron. "After all, we want to make you as comfortable as possible."

"I could use a bottle of whiskey," is what he wanted to say. Instead his body curled in on itself, wracked once again with a fit of coughing. He grabbed at a small white handkerchief that sat on his bedside table and used it to cover his mouth. When the coughing subsided and he pulled the cloth away, he found it flecked with blood. More blood than usual. Not a good sign, though not surprising either.

The nurse placed a cold hand to his forehead and made soothing noises meant to comfort and reassure. He knew she meant well, but he hated her for it, despite her intentions. He understood that she knew that in end, there would be nothing that she, or anyone in the sanitarium for that matter, could do for him. His fate was sealed. It was only a matter of time. Yet they all continued to go through the motions, trying to make his remaining time comfortable and free of worry. And for that he would curse them with his last remaining breath. He didn't need their pity, their fuss, or their bother. He wanted to be out there, in the saloons, a winning hand on the table and guns blazing away. He wanted to be free. As he had it now, he might as well have been in prison.

The coughing fit passed and the nurse continued with her morning routine. She fluffed his pillow, fussed him out of bed long enough to use the chamber pot, had him sit in a chair by the window as she changed his bedding, and forced him to listen to her prattle on and on about any little piece of information that popped into her empty head.

Soon it was time to get back into bed. As he lay back, he looked down at his feet. After everything he had been through, after all he'd seen, all he'd done, he would die with his boots off. He smiled at the irony.

"The doctor will be in to see you later this afternoon. In the meantime, is there anything I can do for you?" the nurse asked as she tucked the fresh linens in around him, trapping him in the bed.

"How about a bottle of whisky?" he asked.

"You know we can't allow that," she replied, a look of sour disappointment crossing her face.

"Damn, this is funny," was all he could say and sent her on her way with a whack on her behind.

There wasn't much to do in the sanitarium, no one visited anymore, he wasn't allowed whisky, and playing solitaire just reminded him of the old days.

All he had left, until death came to claim him, was sleep. He smiled for the second time that morning. Sometimes the irony was just too much.

◆　◆　◆　◆　◆

He woke from the nightmare, sitting bolt upright in bed, a scream lodged in his throat. He looked around the room in panic, groping at his side for the pistols that were no longer there. He was alone.

He lay back on the pillow, the memory of the dream fading. He tried to bring it back, but he might as well have been trying to grab at smoke. There was a bear, he could remember that, a giant grizzly bear. It stood over him, clawing and biting in a frenzy.

Ripping into his clothes, his flesh, his soul. That's when he woke and found himself back in the sanitarium.

The room was dark. He'd slept most of the day. The coughing took him again, bending his body into an unnatural position. It came on so swiftly and with such ferocity that he didn't get a chance to snatch his handkerchief from the table. He didn't even bother covering his mouth and instead let the blood spray the pristine white of his blankets.

The coughing abated and he laid back, thinking that he might go back to sleep. Hoping that this time he wouldn't wake.

"That was a bad one," a voice said from the front of the room.

He sat up to find a man in a suit standing in the doorway, the light from the hall spilling over him.

The man's suit was black, even the shirt. A black bowler hat sat perched at a jaunty angle atop the man's head.

"You the new doctor?" he asked the stranger.

"No," the man in black smiled. "I am not a doctor."

"What do you want?"

"I need to talk to you, John."

John. No one had called him that in a great long time. "Then talk. I'm afraid I can't guarantee you that I'll survive the conversation."

The man in black smiled again. He had a thick black mustache that hung down on each side of his mouth. When the dark man smiled the mustache moved. It looked to John like a black worm that wriggled about on his lip. Something about the man gave John a feeling of darkness, of foreboding. He didn't care for it.

"You aren't doing too good, John," the man in black said, stepping into the room and approaching the bed. "I don't think you are much longer for this life."

"I got doctors to tell me the obvious. What do you want?" he asked.

"John," the man in black sat at the edge of the bed and looked down at him. "What if I told you that I could make you better? What if I told you that I could take the sickness away? That you could go back to gambling? That you could go back to being you?"

"How do you expect to do that?" he asked, a bitter smile on his lips. "You some kind of preacher? You gonna tell me that all I have to do is confess my sins and ask for forgiveness and then I'll be allowed to walk through the gates of Heaven and all will be as it was?"

"No, John," the man in black laughed. "I'm no preacher. Well, not in the way you might define it."

The man in black smiled again and John saw something in his eyes. Something that wasn't quite ... right. A touch of something unnatural. The look held no compassion. The look held nothing but contempt. Not just for John, but for everything. The bed, the room, even the world beyond. The man's eyes reached out and took hold of him. Pulled him in. Captivated him. The eyes managed to be both comforting and disturbing, causing a chill to race through him.

"Who are you?" John asked, his voice nothing more than a whisper.

"I'm the one who can help you, John. The only one. I can return you to your glory. Imagine it. Imagine it, John. Imagine being back in the saloons. A winning hand, a shot of whisky, the women, the fear you inspired in people. Now imagine it without this sickness eating you up from the inside out. Imagine it, John."

"It sounds nice," he said, his voice sounding distant to his own ears as he gazed deep into the man's eyes.

"I can do that for you, John. Me. Only me."

"How?" he asked. "How can you do that?"

"Just know that I can, John. Do you believe me? Do you believe that I can do this for you? Do you believe in me?"

"I do. I do believe," he said. He began to feel light-headed. His head was floating gently like a wisp of smoke as he lost himself in the man's dark eyes.

"Then that leaves us with only one question, John."

"What? What question?"

"How much, John? What would you give to go back? To go back without the sickness and do it all over again? How much would you pay?"

"Everything," he whispered, he floated. "Anything."

"I have some paperwork here, John. You see?" The dark man held out a short stack of papers. Papers filled with words written in thick, black ink. Words that looked to be written in an alien or long dead language. The words were scrawled across the pages in such a way that they seemed to be alive, crawling and wriggling around the papers in desperate impatience. But John didn't see any of this. John hadn't moved. He refused to break his gaze. His eyes stayed connected with the eyes of the man in black.

"Yes," he said. "Yes, I see."

"All I need from you is your signature, John. Just that. Your signature, right here on this line," the man gestured to a line at the bottom of the paper.

"My signature?" he asked dreamily. "That's it?"

"That's it, John." The man in black placed a pen in his hand. "Just sign, John. Just sign right here and everything will change."

John signed, never taking his eyes off of the dark man. He just signed the paper, his hand moving on its own, a smile of ecstasy forming on his face.

"Good, John. Good," the man in black said as he rolled up the paperwork and stood. "Now, just go back to sleep. Sleep for the last time. And when you wake, all will be different. When you wake, you will be yourself again."

"Myself, again," John said. Then he yawned and closed his eyes.

Soon he was snoring, his blankets pulled up to his chin. The man in black remained. Watching. Waiting.

John's breathing slowed. The dark man waited.

John coughed weakly. The dark man watched.

John's heart stopped. The dark man smiled.

"Now we shall see," the man in black said to the empty room. "Now we shall see."

◆　◆　◆　◆　◆

Three hours after the last breath had escaped John's body, as the early morning sun began to filter in through the frost covered windows, a girl entered the room and approached John's bed.

She looked to be about six or seven and wore a plain wool dress that was a gray so dark in color that it was practically black. In general she was a thoroughly unremarkable little girl. She did however, have two odd peculiarities about her.

The first was a large five pointed star that was sewn upon the front of her dress, right smack in the center. The star was made from a fabric so white that it seemed to glow and pulse with its own inner light.

Her second peculiarity was her hair. It was a shade of brown that was quite common and nothing to write home about, but had been done up in no less than seven pony tails that stuck up in random points atop her head, the rest hanging to just above her shoulders.

The little girl looked upon John's lifeless form with sadness as she placed a hand to his brow.

A tear rolled slowly down her cheek and landed upon the star on her chest.

The little girl removed her hand from John's brow and placed it upon his still chest, resting there for only a moment before she let it drop back to her side.

"Don't worry, John," she said, her voice a whisper. "I'm not ready to give up on you just yet."

She turned her back on John's body and made her way back across the room to the door, moving in an effortless manner, virtually floating across the wooden floor.

She stopped at the threshold and smiled, turning to look back at John once more from over her shoulder.

"It's never too late, John. It's never too late."

And with that, she was gone.

CHAPTER ONE

O NCE UPON A TIME, in the small town of Grimmelton, Kansas, there lived three bears.

These were no ordinary bears, mind you. They didn't live in caves, they didn't stand about by great North American rivers, idly swiping salmon from the churning waters as the poor fish struggled upstream in hopes of perpetuating their species, and they most certainly did not spend the greater part of their day trying to steal honey from bees.

No, these bears were different.

These bears walked upright, used tools with opposable thumbs, spoke English with ease, wore the most fashionable clothing, and drove only the finest of automobiles. They attended high society functions and ate at the most expensive restaurants.

But these bears, despite their discernable tastes, were no snobs. They gave great swaths of money to varying charities and volunteered most nights at the local soup kitchen where they laughed and made merry with all who walked through the doors. They were well loved and respected by many in the community, and the three bears reciprocated in kind, regardless of station or financial standing.

Burt Abraham Griswold, patriarch of this family of bears, crept silently across the freshly mown grass of his front lawn with a rifle in his hand. Burt was worried and fearful. Only one round remained in the rifle. One round, and no spares in his pack. He tried to remain optimistic. One round and the right opportunity was all Burt needed to take his son out and end what the boy had started once and for all.

Burt crouched behind a hedgerow. He checked to make sure the gun was loaded properly. The hedges stretched out on either side of him, making a wall that lined the graveled walk which led to the front door of his house. Burt figured that it was just a matter of time before his son, Danny, came up the walk. Then, he would strike.

The position of the sun in the sky had changed slightly from when he began, which told Burt that this little campaign had gone on for over an hour now. Too long. He knew that he had to end it. He just needed to be patient.

A few minutes passed. The only sounds Burt could hear were the calls of birds, cars speeding down Walter Road, and a lawn mower somewhere in the distance. He checked the rifle once again.

Burt knew about guns from his tour in the war, but this one was strange to his hands. It didn't fit quite right, but it was all he had. He would have to make due.

Soon Burt heard the distinct sound of gravel crunching under foot. It was time. He tensed as the footsteps drew near. Burt didn't dare to look over the top of the hedge, but he knew the sound could only mean one thing. Danny, walking up the gravel path toward the house, just as Burt knew he would.

Burt tensed, ready to spring when the moment came. He rested a finger on the trigger and pressed the rifle's stock back against his shoulder. As the footsteps came to a point just on the other side of the hedgerow where Burt waited, he popped up like a jack-in-the-box, and squeezed the trigger.

Burt hit his target, but it wasn't his son. It wasn't Danny. It was a woman.

Burt had to stifle a laugh at the sight of Mrs. Sugarbaker with a suction cup dart sticking dead center to her forehead.

"It looks like you got me, Mr. Griswold," Henrietta Sugarbaker said, her voice the essence of restrained fury.

"I'm so sorry about that, Henrietta," Burt said, still fighting to hold back his laughter. "I thought you were Danny."

"Do I look like your son?" She asked, her eyes narrowing at the familiar use of her first name.

Burt knew better then to answer. He could spot a rhetorical question at three hundred yards.

"Have you, maybe, seen Danny at all this morning, Mrs. Sugarbaker? You know, while you were out taking care of things?"

"No, Mr. Griswold," said Mrs. Sugarbaker, head of grounds keeping for Griswold House, and all around sour pickle. "I have not seen young Danny. I have a feeling, however," she continued, pulling the dart from her forehead with an audible pop before handing it over to Burt, "that he will see you, before you see him."

That's when Burt heard a faint click and felt something small hit him in the back of the head. Something like a suction cup dart.

"Gotcha!" a voice shouted from behind him.

Mrs. Sugarbaker gave Burt a sly wink and walked on up the path toward the house. Burt turned to find a large tooth-filled smile with his son, Danny, standing behind it.

"I gotcha, Dad!" he shouted as he started to dance in place right there on the grass.

"What are you doing?" Burt laughed.

"I'm doing my 'I Beat My Dad Happy Dance'," Danny replied, still dancing.

"That looks a lot like your 'Macaroni and Cheese Happy Dance'," Burt said, walking over to this son and putting an arm around his shoulder.

"Well yeah," Danny said, "It's the only dance I know."

Danny was nine years old and, for the moment, an only child. Burt was often amazed at how his life had changed once Danny was born. Everything he had once thought important in life took a back seat once the child had entered his life.

A small beep sounded from the watch on Danny's right wrist and the boy took a quick look at the numbers on the face.

"It's twelve o'clock, Dad," Danny started to rock back and forth while bouncing slightly. "Mom said we had to be back in by twelve. We gotta go. We gotta go!" His voice had raised in pitch as he tugged on Burt's hand.

"Okay, pal. Okay," Burt let himself be pulled along behind the cub.

◆　◆　◆　◆　◆

Burt Griswold often liked to joke that he had made all of his money by investing in salmon futures. One particular salmon, actually. Simon the Salmon had more talent in his dorsal fin than most folks had in their entire bloodline.

Burt liked to think that God had been smiling down upon him that day at the county fair. Burt had been wandering among the tents and carnival barkers – on a quest to find the funnel cake stand – when he had come across the strangest site he'd ever seen. In an out of the way place, on the very outskirts of the fair, was a small stage. Standing atop the stage was an even smaller salmon. Simon the Salmon.

Simon's entire body was covered by a special suit that allowed him to breathe out of water. In the center of the suit, over what would have been the fish's chest, if fishes were said to have chests, was a small speaker. Perched on the stage, directly in front of the speaker, was a microphone on a stand.

Burt watched in awe as Simon the Salmon performed his standup comedy routine for a small group of onlookers, most of whom were fairgoers on their way from the parking area to the main fairgrounds. Burt noticed right away that those who had stopped to see this little fish were laughing, rather hysterically. Furthermore, in just moments, what had been nothing more than a small gathering of rubberneckers, quickly turned into a respectable mass of laughing fans.

Burt had never laughed so hard in his entire life, and so he had found himself doing something he'd never thought he'd do. He sought out Simon the Salmon and signed him up for a management contract right there on the spot. It was a standard management agreement. Burt would set up the appearances and get ten percent of everything Simon made.

Using a bit of luck and a few contacts from his time in the military, Burt managed to get Simon booked into comedy clubs all across the country. It wasn't long before the nation saw what Burt had known deep in his gut. Simon the Salmon was funny. It was soon after that Simon had been offered a supporting role in a television sitcom.

The show had been a critical success. However, as it had aired on Fox, it was cancelled after just four episodes. Neither Burt nor Simon were dismayed. Burt kept booking gigs and Simon kept traveling the country, making people laugh.

Then Burt landed Simon a two picture deal with a major movie studio. The first movie featured Simon as the comic relief in a Kurt Steel action flick. It had bombed, but of course, most Kurt Steel movies did. The studio however, had loved Simon in the role and took a chance on his next picture, which Simon wrote himself. That summer, Simon the Salmon and the Slippery Seal of Salisbury broke box office records all across the world. Simon the Salmon quickly became a household name and went on to make seven consecutive box office smashes in a row. The Griswold family was set for life, all thanks to Burt's keen sense of humor.

Simon's success brought about financial independence for Burt and his lovely bride Beatrice, especially as the two looked to add a child to the family, the child that would be Danny. With financial independence came the Griswold's desire to build, to lay down some roots, and to help others.

With that in mind, Burt had hired as many out of work builders, carpenters, plumbers, electricians, and general laborers as he could find, and set them to the task of building his family a house. The work soon became such an immense task that it had revitalized Grimmelton's floundering economy and helped save more than one family from starvation and ruin.

When the last nailed had been pounded, the paint dried, and the dust all but settled, what stood was an architectural marvel, a sprawling mansion covering over 180,000 square feet and boasting no less than 260 rooms. The people of Grimmelton dubbed the building, Griswold House, though to label such a structure as nothing more than a mere house would be like referring to the Sistine Chapel as just another church.

With construction complete, the Griswolds were free to hire housekeepers, groundskeepers, cooks, security personnel, and pretty much anyone else who could help maintain the palatial estate and keep things running smoothly.

The Griswolds were kind and generous employers. They gave every employee a chance to make something more out of their lives. Working for the Griswold's didn't just mean a steady paycheck. It meant health benefits, a retirement plan, paid vacations and holidays, even a tuition reimbursement plan for employees who wanted to get their degree. Working for the Griswold Family soon became the most sought after job in town.

To the community, Griswold House was an industry. For the Griswolds, it was home.

◆　◆　◆　◆　◆

Burt and Danny found Beatrice in her office on the second floor. She was at her desk, glasses perched atop her head, typing away furiously at her laptop.

"How's the book coming?" Burt asked as Danny leaped into his mother's arms with wild abandon, nearly knocking her from the chair.

"You're getting too big to keep doing that," Beatrice said to the boy with a laugh in her voice. She pulled Danny to her, returning the fierce love that he had put into his hug.

"What?" she asked, smiling up at Burt as Danny attempted to burrow his way through her chest and into her heart with the top of his head.

"What?" Burt asked back.

"You said something. I missed it because your son was using me as a tackling dummy."

"You're not a dummy," Danny said, his voice muffled by the crook of his mother's neck.

"I just asked how the book was coming," Burt said, sitting on a couch along the wall.

"Oh it's coming, you know, one-"

"Word at a time," Burt finished the line for her and laughed.

"Yeah," Beatrice laughed with him. "I guess I've used that little chestnut a few times."

"Just a couple times," Burt smiled.

"Mom, it's after Noon," Danny began to bounce in her lap. "It's after Noon, Mom. After Noon."

Beatrice checked her watch. "It sure is. I guess we better hit the road."

Danny giggled. "Hit the road."

Burt smiled again. He knew that Danny had formed a picture in his head, imagining for a moment all three of them standing out on the road in front of the house, pounding their fists into the pavement.

"Hit the road," Danny repeated. "We gotta hit the road. It's after Noon."

Each afternoon, as the chef prepared lunch, the Griswolds went for a walk around town. This was all part of their daily routine and they stuck to it for Danny's sake. Danny didn't do well with interruptions in his routine. The destination varied each day. It didn't matter much to Danny exactly where they walked to, as long as they didn't miss the walk itself.

The smell of boiling lobster meat rolled slowly around them, causing their collective mouths to water as the three bears made their way through the house and out the front door. Today the chef, Mr. Greengrass, had prepared for them his famous lobster bisque, a meal the Griswold family adored almost as much as they adored Chef Greengrass.

"Can we get some gum?" Danny asked as they set out for their walk.

"Of course, pal," Burt said, ruffling the fur at the top of Danny's head. "We'll walk on down to the store. What do you say, Bea?"

"I think that's a great idea," Beatrice said, taking Danny's hand.

"I think it's a great idea too," Danny said, smiling and hopping.

And so, as the Griswold family set out on that sunny day, with temperatures in the mid-seventies and a gentle breeze blowing from the north, they had no clue, not one iota of an idea that the day would end in anguish, tragedy, destruction, and death.

But then, not all days can be winners.

CHAPTER TWO

A DRIFTER APPEARED IN town.

This wasn't your typical dust-caked, dead-in-the-eyes, home-on-their-back drifter either. No, this drifter looked like she might be more at home dancing the night away in some trendy New York club rather than hoofing it through the back roads of America. But here she was, walking into town with nothing more than a backpack and a mischievous glint in her eyes.

She was dressed appropriately for someone walking the Earth: One pair of black sunglasses, one pair of comfortable black hiking boots, one pair of durable – yet fashionable – khaki cargo pants, one military green canvas backpack flung casually over her right shoulder, and one low cut spaghetti strap black t-shirt. Everything that today's woman needs when drifting across the country.

Yet, despite her somewhat plain appearance, she wore her attire like a diva – nay, a queen. She was the star of the show and all eyes were on her.

The drifter arrived in town with an air of indifference. Nothing impressed her; nothing could when she looked so good. The fact was, compared to her, everything else was vanilla.

She made her way through downtown Grimmelton, turning heads as she strolled through the busy town square. She was a stranger in a strange place, but she held herself as though she owned it all.

The scene was like something out of a big name shampoo commercial. She might as well have been walking in slow motion. Men couldn't keep their eyes off of her. If she dropped her backpack, she knew the area would turn into a cartoon as men fought one another to pick it up for her. They would kill to be the one lucky enough to return to her that which she had lost (and possibly gain her favor).

The knowledge of that made her smile. Her smile made an old main faint, a lecherous grin on his face.

The drifter's name was Lucy, though most folks called her Goldilocks, on account of her hair. Her golden tresses were the admiration of any who saw them. What most folks didn't know however, was that her hair color had come out of a bottle.

Goldilocks had been on the road for over a year, drifting from town to town, no apparent destination in mind, never stopping long in one place, getting by on nothing more than her good looks and a truck load of wits. Unfortunately, good looks and wits only got you so far, and for the moment, Goldilocks realized that she was hungry. So she set off across town to find an out of the way place where she could do her thing and get some grub.

Half an hour later she found herself on the other side of town, a few miles from the city proper. Her tummy grumbled when she noticed a lone convenience store at the foot of a large hill, surrounded by farmland.

The store was called The Brick House Gas and Groceries. It sat at the crossroads of Walter Road and Hickory Lane. Called simply 'The Store' by the locals, the Brick House had been a Grimmelton landmark for the past sixty years. It was owned and operated by the three Pig Brothers; Larry, Gary, and Colin. The store had been in their family for years, going back to the time when their grandfather, Wilbur J. Pig, opened up the place in 1952. Since then, The Brick House Gas and Groceries has been the one place the citizens of Grimmelton could count on to get their gas, and yes, their groceries.

A plan came to mind so Goldilocks stashed her backpack behind a trashcan and entered the store.

Colin had the misfortune to be working the counter that afternoon and, as many a wary woman from within a fifty mile radius knew, he had an eye for the ladies. So he noticed Goldilocks the moment she stepped through the door. It was a slow afternoon, and he put down his *Modern Architecture* magazine and greeted Goldilocks like the player he thought he was.

"Good afternoon, beautiful. Welcome to the Brick House. My name is Colin, and if there is anything I can do for you, anything at all, please let me know. I am at your every beck and call," the words dripped from his mouth like oil from a can. He grinned confidently, not hiding the gaze that looked her over from top to bottom.

Goldilocks pushed her sunglasses to the top of her head, smiled, and approached the counter the way a panther approaches its prey. "I'm sure I can think of something you can do for me," she purred, putting a slight emphasis on the word 'do' and leaning forward over the counter, her eyes twinkling wickedly.

Colin couldn't believe his luck. A platinum blonde party girl, right out of a magazine, standing right before him, and giving him the eye.

Goldilocks couldn't believe her luck. An ignorant pig with delusions of grandeur, standing right before her, and he had control of the store.

"I'm afraid that my car has broken down," she pouted, her lower lip sticking out slightly. "And I lost my purse last night. It had my wallet and my phone in it. I just don't know what to do."

"Is there anyone I can call for you?"

"That's so sweet of you," she said, leaning forward a tad more. "But, I have a friend meeting me here in a couple hours."

"A friend?" Colin looked panicked, worried that the friend might mean a guy.

"Yeah, one of my sorority sisters."

"Sorority?" Colin could have giggled.

"She's coming to pick me up and take me home. But I'm so hungry. I haven't eaten since last night," she pushed her lower lip out even more and added fairly more angle to her frame, providing Colin with such a site to behold.

"Baby," Colin practically danced. "You've come to the right place."

"My name is Goldilocks, by the way," she held out her right hand, palm down.

Colin took her fingers and planted a soft kiss on the back of her hand. "Just tell me how I can help, Goldie."

Colin had this amazing gift of looking at Goldilocks everywhere but her eyes. Goldilocks didn't mind. Actually, she counted on it. Otherwise she wouldn't have been leaning over the counter to give Colin so much look at.

"Do you think you could spare a burrito and a drink for me? My friend can pay you when she gets here. I'm so hungry, and I would be so appreciative, and so would my friend," she smiled and gave her eyebrows a slight flutter.

"Appreciative? How appreciative?"

"Hmm," she said, looking up with a finger on her lower lip. "I think better when I'm not so hungry."

Colin smiled, walked out from behind the counter, grabbed a burrito from the freezer, and put it in the microwave. Goldilocks took a quick survey of the lot through the double glass doors. She could see the entire lot from her vantage point, and the only car in view was a shiny new Chevy Camaro, black with white racing stripes.

"Is that your car?" she asked Colin.

"That's my girl," he said, filling a soda from the fountain.

"I just love fast cars."

Goldilocks threw a quick glance over the counter and spied a set of keys on a ring lying next to the cash register. Attached to the key ring was a small, plastic, novelty license plate. On the license plate she could read the words:

REAL MEN DRIVE FAST

This would be too easy. She almost felt sorry for the pig.

"So," Colin said as he brought Goldilocks her drink. "While we're waiting for your burrito, why don't you tell me a little bit about yourself."

Goldilocks leaned back on the counter. "What do you want to know?"

"Well, first off, you aren't from around here. I'd remember running into you before," Colin leaned in close to her as she sipped her soda through a straw. "Where are you from?"

"I'm from Nunyo."

"You're from where?"

"Nunyo."

"Nunyo?"

"Nunyo."

"I've never heard of Nunyo," Colin said, scratching at the stubble he had growing on on his chinny-chin-chin.

"It's in the southwest," Goldilocks smiled quietly to herself. This pig was a real idiot. He obviously didn't get the joke. Nunyo, as in Nunyo business.

The two stood there for a moment in silence.

"Is the store always this empty?" she asked.

"Oh yeah, this time of day, everyone's working. We should pick up by 12:30 as folks come in for lunch," which was just over twenty minutes away. Goldilocks would have to work fast.

"I like it empty like this," she said, smiling and leaning closer. "I don't know what it is about you Colin. I mean, we just met and everything, and I don't even know you, but I like being alone with you. You make me comfortable."

"Yeah?"

"Oh yeah. I feel like I can let go with you, Colin. You ever feel that way with anyone?"

"Not until now," he leaned in even closer, putting each hand on the counter to either side of her, enveloping her. Her eyes were like pools and Colin took a few laps before he bent in to kiss her.

Before their lips made contact, the microwave dinged, breaking the silence. Goldilocks screamed and jumped, which in turn caused her to drop her cup, which in turn caused Colin to scream and jump and back away as the cup hit the floor, spilling soda all along the linoleum. This was, of course, all part of her plan.

"I'm sorry," she said in a cute, pouting sort of way that always manages to turn men into putty. "The microwave startled me."

"That's okay, baby," Colin moved back in, awkwardly trying to lean in for a kiss while avoiding the spilled soda on the floor. "It ain't nothing but a chicken wing on a string."

"No," she said, pushing him away. "This isn't going to work. I have this thing about spills and messes. They're icky. I can't feel comfortable, I can't – let go – with that on the floor."

"No?"

"No. Would you clean it up for me," she stuck her index finger in her mouth to suck off some of the soda that had spilled there.

Had Colin been a cartoon character, his eyes would have shot three feet out of his eye sockets while a steam whistle popped up out of the top of his head and blew a shrill, steady note. Colin wasn't a cartoon character, but he made a fairly good go of it.

"Sure, sure babe. I'll clean it up in a jiffy," he sprinted to the back of the store, to a door that said "Employees Only".

"Don't be long," she called after him as he launched himself through the door.

As soon as the door closed behind him, Goldilocks vaulted the counter, grabbed the keys, vaulted back, and ran through the double glass, automatic doors and into the parking lot.

She snatched her backpack from behind the trashcan and got behind the wheel of the Camaro. She tore out of the lot, smoke billowing from the tires as she spun out onto the asphalt, leaving two dark lines of burnt rubber.

As she sped out of the lot and onto the two lane that was Walter Road, Colin came running toward her, fear and confusion on his face. She just smiled, smashed the gas pedal to the floor with her foot, and shot up Walter Road at over eighty miles an hour, passing three bears who looked to be out for a leisurely stroll.

In her rush to get a set of wheels, Goldilocks forgot all about the burrito. She was still hungry and needed to eat. Going back for the food would be foolhardy. She'd have to find something else. Some other poor sucker to con out of food, money, or both. She always did.

Goldilocks roared up Walter Road, which took her back into town. She figured she would drive the back roads as much as possible to avoid the interstate and the police. As she crested the hill that made up most of Walter Road, she spied a sprawling mansion off on the horizon. It stood alone. The sun shone behind it, causing the house to glow in an angelic light.

She stopped the car, got out, and stood on the side of the empty road, looking up at the house. This was a place to get a decent bite to eat. Heck, if she played it right, she might even have a place to stay for the next couple of days, and leave with some money in her pocket to boot.

First she'd have to ditch the car. Stash it someplace where no one would find it, but also a place where she could come back and get it, just in case.

Next, she'd have to beat herself up some. After all, no one can resist a damsel in distress.

CHAPTER THREE

A THICK FOGBANK OF scents rolled slowly through the Griswold's massive kitchen. Lobster, onions, and a hint of tomato. Jack inhaled deeply, filling his nasal passages with the heavenly aroma as he sat at an out-of-the-way counter, snacking on crackers and cheese and reading a book.

To say that the Griswold's kitchen was a hive of activity would only belittle the military precision that took place each day in the cavernous maze of stainless steel. Scores of men and women – dressed in white – scurried here and there, knives flying, spoons swirling, all under the scrutiny of Chef Michael Greengrass.

"You need a refill there, Jack?" asked Chef Greengrass.

Jack had been nursing a diet soda for the last fifteen minutes. "Oh, no thanks, Mike," he replied, looking up from his book.

Jack liked Mike Greengrass. Of course, it was hard to dislike such a man. Mike ruled his kitchen with an iron spoon, yet was always kind and fair. In truth, Jack considered Mike to be his closest, if not his only friend, and figured Mike felt the same toward him.

"Whatcha reading there?" the chef asked, wiping his hands on his apron.

Jack handed the hardback over to Mike and took a sip of his soda.

"The new Jack Reacher," Mike said in awe as he read through the synopsis on the inside cover.

Jack loved to read. He also loved to follow the adventures of characters who shared his name. Jack Reacher, Jack Ryan, or Jack Bauer, it didn't matter. He just enjoyed the fantasy. He liked to imagine himself as the hero. The only one willing to take a stand. To do what needed to be done to protect the innocent masses who probably didn't even understand that they were in any danger.

"It any good?" Mike asked as he handed the book back.

"So far," Jack replied. He wanted to elaborate, but was interrupted by a voice in his ear that only Jack could hear.

"Jack, this is Stan at the main door. You copy?"

"Just a moment, Mike" Jack said, holding a finger to his left ear.

The voice spoke from a small speaker in Jack's right ear, the cord twisting back behind the ear and down into his suit jacket.

Jack stood and spoke into the cuff of his sleeve, "Go for Jack."

"Jack, we got a young lady here at the main door. Claims she was carjacked. She's asked to use the phone."

"She injured?"

"Minor injuries. Cuts, scrapes, possible bruising. Nothing life threatening."

"Okay," Jack paused, looking around at the activity in the kitchen as he thought it through. "Have Keith bring her to me in the kitchen. And send Melanie after them. I'll sort it out."

"Copy, Jack. They will be with you momentarily."

"Problem?" Mike asked.

"Not really," Jack related his conversation.

"Anything I can do to help?" Mike asked.

"Thanks, Mike, but no." Jack gulped down his soda. "You can have someone clear this stuff away if you really want to help." Jack smiled.

"Sure thing, pal," Mike said, and cleared it away himself.

Jack smiled again as he watched Mike carry his stuff away. Mike wasn't the kind of guy who would ask someone else to do something that he was perfectly capable of doing himself.

Jack brushed the cracker crumbs from his tie and adjusted the Beretta in his shoulder holster. It was a thing with Jack, periodically adjusting his side arm. Not because wearing it was uncomfortable, which it wasn't, but mainly just to reassure himself that it was still there.

Mike always poked fun at Jack for taking his job too seriously. Being the head of security for the Griswold Family didn't entail much in the way of, well … security. Grimmelton had been in the record books for generations for having the lowest crime rate of any city of like population in the world, but Jack knew better. He had been in the war. Jack had seen and done things he would never forget. Things that twist his dreams and weigh heavy on his soul. He knew that there was still darkness in the world, even in Grimmelton.

It's why he had always had the family shadowed when they went out for their afternoon walks. Jack *tried* to send a security team out with the Griswold's whenever they left the house. No, the family wasn't royalty, nor was Mr. Griswold the President. It was rather unlikely that the family would be the target of a kidnapping, assassination, or simple random mugging. But the family paid Jack to keep them safe, and by God that's just what he would do.

Besides, he'd grown to like the Griswolds, and they him. He was practically family, and Jack was raised to cherish family.

So even though Mr. Griswold insisted that he and the family could take a walk about town without five or six of Jack's guys watching out for them every step of the way, Jack sent a team out anyway. The Griswolds were just unaware that his team was there.

Soon Keith arrived in the kitchen with a young blonde woman, and for a moment Jack found himself speechless. The woman was stunning.

For a few moments, nothing happened. Jack found that he wasn't able to make himself talk. Jack was typically uncomfortable around women. He found them strange and difficult to understand. Jack was even more uncomfortable around attractive women. So for a moment or two, just long enough for the silence to become real and truly awkward, Jack just stood and stared.

"Sir?" Keith said, breaking Jack from his spell.

Jack was about to reply when something about this woman caught his eye. Maybe it was his imagination, but while she looked as frightened as a caged deer, Jack swore he could see something else in her eyes. Something like ... triumph?

"Sir?" Keith said again, and once more Jack was back from within his head and whatever it was Jack thought he saw was gone.

"Thanks, Keith," Jack said, clearing his throat to try and mask the awkward moment. "You're dismissed."

"Thank you, sir," Keith nearly saluted before walking away.

Jack then turned to the woman. "I'm Jack Horner," he said, offering the woman his hand. "I'm head of security."

She looked at his hand with unmasked anxiety and Jack could see that she shook visibly as her eyes darted around the kitchen like a scared mouse.

"Are you okay, ma'am?"

"Oh," she seemed quite startled by the question. "Yes, I'm sorry. It's just," she paused. Jack thought for a moment that she might cry. Crying women made Jack even more uncomfortable than attractive women did. "It's just been an incredibly bad day. Horrifying, really," she smiled meekly.

"Melanie should be here in a moment to see to your injuries. She's a registered nurse. In the meantime, please have a seat," Jack gestured to the stool he had been sitting on just minutes ago.

She thanked him and sat. She almost didn't make it. To Jack it looked like she might faint, but in the end she sat and began to look more relaxed.

"Can you tell me what happened?" Jack asked.

"Oh, goodness. It all went down so fast. I don't even know what happened. I had stopped at a stop sign, then there was a gun in my face and this man was screaming at me, and then," she started to cry. "And then, he," her crying became more frantic. She buried her face in her hands.

"It's okay," Jack said soothingly, handing her his handkerchief. "Everything is going to be okay. Once I call the Police, you can give them a description of this guy, and then you can maybe get your car back."

"The Police?" she said, raising her head. "No, please, don't call the Police."

Jack was confused. "Why wouldn't I call the Police? You were attacked."

"I just need to use the phone," she sniffed and then blew her nose. "I have a sister in the area who can come get me. I need to get back home. I have a job interview waiting for me."

"But, what about your car?"

"It was a rental."

"Ma'am, I can't let you go without talking to the Police. The rental company will need a Police report."

"I can't," she began to cry again. "I can't talk to the Police. I just can't."

"Ma'am, please," Jack laid a hand gently on her shoulder.

"No!" she screamed, slapping his hand away and leaping off the stool, cringing back from Jack as if he were something from a nightmare.

The stool that Goldilocks had been sitting on clattered to the floor, echoing into what Jack realized was the silence her shout had caused as the entire kitchen crew stopped what they were doing to see what the trouble was.

"Everything okay, Jack," Mike asked, drying his hands on his apron as he approached cautiously, a look of concern on his face.

"Yeah, everything's great," Jack said, pulling the stool from the floor and placing it upright. "The young lady and I were just having a conversation and she got a little excited. Isn't that right, Miss ..."

"Goldilocks," she said, hugging herself and shivering. "Call me Goldilocks."

CHAPTER FOUR

H E WAS KNOWN AS the Beast, and yet he was by far one of the most attractive men in the known world. His chestnut brown hair blew about in the breeze. Despite its length – which hung to the shoulders – his hair never obscured his vision nor kept anyone from seeing his striking face, which somehow managed to be both smooth and rugged at the same time. His eyes, the piercing blue of glass cleaner, had been known to make Clint Eastwood weep with just a look. He walked with an athletic grace that would make a panther green with envy and his smile could make Cleopatra rise from the dead.

The Beast dressed in an expensive dark brown suit and tie. The jacket he'd left behind due to the sword that rode upon his back. The sword, a katana, was an ancient blade with a rich history. The sword, like its bearer, has seen more than its fair share of combat and has spilled blood on three continents. Along with the sword, a revolver that looked too big to believe rode snuggly in a holster under his left arm. There were surely other weapons hidden about his person, but only those with the determination to give up breathing for a living ever got the chance to see them.

The man known as the Beast is – among other things – a warrior, a tracker, and a hunter. His keen, tactical mind had the reputation to be as cold and unfeeling as the bitter Arctic nights, and it has always been a well-known fact that he is at his happiest only among blood, death, devastation, war, and horror. He is an army unto himself. He has toppled governments and ended revolutions. He has abducted queens and defended presidents. In the most general of senses, the Beast is the one man you don't want to mess with, and he was now in the town of Grimmelton, Kansas for only one purpose: To find Goldilocks.

The Beast stood in the middle of Walter Road, gazing at the structure that was the Brick House Gas and Groceries. He sniffed the air curiously, ignoring the cars that honked as they sped past him, missing him by inches. Goldilocks had been here. He had followed her trail through the parking lot and up to the squat little store. He stopped to sniff the air again. He could sense that Goldilocks had entered the store. He could also sense that she hadn't stayed long. He needed to determine what she had been doing in the Brick House Gas and Groceries and where she had gone from here. Her scent leaving the store had already started to fade, which meant she left fast. He knew the direction, but it would speed the process up somewhat if he also knew the destination. The Beast would need to see if the clerk knew anything. And if the clerk wasn't willing to talk … well, they always talked in the end.

The entire front of the store was glass so the Beast paused, standing off to the side of the entrance, and scanned the interior. The lot was empty of cars, but he wanted to make sure that he would be alone with the clerk. An electronic ping sounded in the store as he walked in through the double glass doors and went directly to the counter where a pig stood. The pig had his back to the counter and appeared to be crying softy.

"You got a restroom in this place?" he asked.

"In the back," the pig replied without turning around.

The Beast did a quick check of the restrooms and found them unoccupied. Then he returned to the pig at the counter.

"You alone in here?" he asked.

"What?" the pig turned and looked up at him.

The two stood staring at each other for a moment. The Beast pulled a pack of Lucky Strike non-filtered cigarettes from his pocket, shook one out, plucked it into his mouth, and lit it with a Zippo he produced from another pocket.

"There's no smoking in the store," the pig said before blowing his nose.

"Where's the girl?" the Beast asked.

"You can't smoke in the store."

The Beast smiled. Of all the things for the pig to be concerned about, his gun and sword to name but two, the pig was worried about secondhand smoke. But, no one had ever said he wasn't reasonable, so he threw the cigarette to the floor and ground it out with his boot. He continued to smile as he pulled the pistol, pointed it at the pig's face, and thumbed back the hammer.

"I'm in no mood for killing today," he said, his voice like gravel being drug across a road of sandpaper. "Why don't you just tell me what the girl wanted, and where she went, otherwise I'm eating bacon tonight."

The pig froze.

"Hey, pig," he said. "I'm talking to you."

Colin just stood there, transfixed, staring down the barrel of the revolver. Colin couldn't speak. A deep fear of death had caused his body to go rigid and his mind to escape to a better place.

"Piggy-piggy!" the Beast yelled.

Colin was immobile.

The Beast began to regret pulling the gun. He had no intention of shooting this pig. No, that would draw too much attention. But typically, when he pulled a gun on someone, they tended to talk. Actually, in most cases, they wound up telling him more than he needed. The pig, on the other hand, wasn't playing ball.

He had to try something different, so the Beast put his gun away.

"Look here, buddy-boy. I'm putting my gun away, okay. I'm not going to shoot you, I just need you to answer a question or two."

Colin didn't blink.

The Beast sighed and looked around for anything that might help. That's when he noticed a small set of thick wire shelves full of candy bars and single serve bags of potato chips. They were within reach, so he snatched a bag of chips and threw it at Colin.

The bag bounced harmlessly off of the top of Colin's head.

The Beast grabbed up a candy bar, a hefty and dense Chunky bar, which was less of a bar, and more of a solid square paperweight with sharp corners. He flicked it at Colin like a throwing star. It too bounced off the pig's head with no apparent harm.

The Beast swore. Colin remained a statue. The Beast began scooping up chips and candy bars and hurling them at the pig. Colin was resolute.

This continued for a full ten minutes – the Beast yelling obscenities and pelting Colin with candy bars and bags of potato chips – Colin standing stock-still as candy bars and bags of potato chips bounced harmlessly off of him.

At one point during this ten minute tirade, a customer walked into the store, stopping just inside the threshold as she caught sight of poor Colin and the desperately handsome, candy-throwing, maniac. The customer was Laura Hood, a woman in her early twenties who wore a bright red hoodie, and had come to the store simply to buy some medicine for her grandmother, who lay in bed at home with a nasty head cold. Miss Hood couldn't quite compute the scene before her as she watched the most beautiful man she'd ever seen pelt Colin Pig with various items found on the shelves around him. Her confusion lasted but only a moment, and it became quickly obvious that the Brick House Gas and Groceries may not be the place she wanted to be at the moment. So, she turned and strode from the store, remembering that one of the seven dwarves – Doc, probably – had recently opened a 24-hour pharmacy just on the other side of town. She rode quickly away on her little red scooter, the drama she'd witnessed in the Brick House fleeing from her brain as she left our tale, never to return.

Not long after Laura Hood fled, the Beast determined that he would either have to shoot the pig or try a different tactic. He couldn't get anything out of a dead pig, so shooting him was out of the question. And he needed what information the pig had. The Beast had easily tracked Goldilocks to the store, and he could see, sense actually, that she left. He could sense her right up to a certain point in the parking lot, where her trail just simply disappeared right where a pair of burnt tire tracks started. She obviously got into a car. He couldn't sense a trail once they were in an automobile.

So the Beast slapped Colin hard across the face.

"Ow!" Colin said, bringing a hand up to cradle his cheek.

"Look, friend. I do apologize. I'm afraid I've behaved horribly. I've been rude, I've made a mess of your store, and I assaulted you, but I need some information and I believe that you're the only one that has it," the Beast managed to sound contrite. "I'll tell you what. How about I pick all this up, then you and I can have a little talk? I just need to know where the girl went."

"The g-g-girl?" Colin stammered.

"That's right. Blonde. Smoking hot. Maybe a little manipulative?"

"Goldilocks," Colin started to come out of it.

"That's the girl."

"The witch stole my baby."

"I'm sorry?" Confusion showed on the Beast's face, this was quite unexpected.

"She stole my baby."

"She actually *stole* your baby? Your, uh ... piglet?"

"No, my car. The witch stole my car."

"Ah, okay. Your car. You said she stole your baby and I thought – well, it doesn't matter. Which way did she go?"

"East. She took my car east, toward Griswold House," Colin had begun to weep again.

"Rest easy, son. I'll find her, and your baby."

"You really mean it, mister?"

"You bet your curly tail I do."

The Beast left Colin alone with the mess. Sure, he said he'd help the pig clean the place up, but he was the Beast … and beasts lie.

CHAPTER FIVE

ALL DANNY COULD THINK of as he strolled down Walter Road with his mom and dad was gum. He not only wanted gum, he *needed* gum.

Everyone had always told Danny Griswold that he was a good kid. Teachers, relatives, other kids at school, and all the nice people that worked in his house seemed to genuinely like Danny, which was good, because Danny genuinely liked them right back. Danny was in the 5th grade, and while he flourished academically, he had a few social issues. Danny's mom and dad have told him, on more than one occasion, that Danny's social issues weren't really his fault. They told him that he had autism. Actually, they would clarify that while he had autism, he was "high functioning". Danny wasn't sure what that meant. When his mom and dad would talk about Danny and his autism and being "high functioning" he would often picture himself working with his Lego bricks somewhere up in a tree or on the top of the house because he just figured that you had to be somewhere up high to be high functioning.

Danny has also been told that he is a "sensory seeker", which he knows is just a fancy way of saying that he likes to chew on stuff. He chews on his clothes, his hands, his toys, pretty much anything that is handy and within reach. His mom and dad have talked to him over and over about chewing on stuff. He's put holes in his clothes, he's chewed his fingers till they've bled, and he's bitten his toys into complete uselessness.

That's what made gum so wonderful. He could chew to his heart's content and meet that sensory need while he fed his taste buds flavor at the same time. Besides, didn't four out of five dentists recommend chewing sugar free gum to help promote healthy teeth?

"Dad, don't forget about the gum?" Danny said as the three bears stepped off of the black top of Walter Road and onto the gravel of the Brick House Gas and Groceries parking lot. "You said we could get some gum?"

"Don't worry bud," Burt ruffled the fur on the top of Danny's head. "Gum is just but a few steps away."

As the Griswolds walked across the parking lot of the Brick House, Danny found his attention being pulled to a man who had just come out of the store. The man was unmistakably handsome, even Danny could see that, but the man's extreme attractiveness was not what drew Danny's attention. It was the sword the man wore on his back.

Without warning, Danny's father stopped and held his arm out protectively in front of Danny and his mom. Danny knew his dad didn't like the man with the sword. Danny could feel his dad tense, the muscles in his arm going taut as he stood between his family and what his dad must have felt was a threat to those he held most dear.

"Burt?" his mom asked, trying to move out around him.

"Stay where you're at, Bea," his dad said, watching the man warily.

Danny knew the man wasn't going to hurt him or his mom or dad. He wasn't sure how he knew, he just did, just as he knew that telling his dad that everything would be okay wouldn't do any good. Besides, the man with the sword wasn't even looking in their direction. He just stood there by the entrance to the store, looking up Walter Road, and ... sniffing the air. Danny thought that was funny, but before he could laugh, he noticed the man's hair. Danny was transfixed by it. The man's hair stirred slightly in the gentle breeze, yet not once did the man's hair obscure his face. Not even for a second. It was as if the man with the sword kept his hair out of his face by sheer force of will. It was ... magical.

But then the man with the sword disappeared. He just seemed to meld into nothingness. One moment the man was there, standing and sniffing the air, and the next moment the man turned slightly to one side, and vanished.

"Cool!" Danny said excitedly. "He's magic!"

"Um," was all his dad seemed to be able to muster.

"I'm sure he just walked around to the back of the store," his mom said, smiling.

"Yeah," his dad said. "I'm sure that's where he went."

"Can we get gum now?" Danny asked, shaking his head. Danny knew what he saw. The man used magic to teleport himself away from the parking lot of the Brick House.

"Sure, pal," his dad said, laughing. But Danny could tell that his dad's laugh was a lie. His dad was worried. So was his mom. He could feel it in their hands as they each took one of his.

"It's okay," Danny said. "That man doesn't want to hurt us. He's just looking for something."

"Of course he is, pal," his dad laughed again. "That guy is long gone. Got nothing to do with us."

Danny just smiled. He knew telling his parents that it was okay wouldn't do any good, but Danny knew in some sense that it was the parent's job to worry, so Danny let them worry ... just as long as he was able to get some gum.

Yet, his dad didn't move. He just stood there looking at where the handsome man disappeared.

"Dad?" Danny asked. "Gum?"

"Burt, are you alright?" his mom said.

"Yeah," his dad said. "Yeah, I'm fine," he gave a snort of laughter. "I'm fine, let's get Danny some gum."

Danny let out a little cheer of joy in his head as the set off through the parking lot.

The first thing the Griswolds found as they walked into the Brick House Gas and Groceries was the mess. The three bears paused just inside the sliding glass doors and looked with confusion at the candy bars and potato chip bags that were strewn about on the floor before the counter.

That's when Danny heard the distinct sound of a pig crying and saw Colin Pig behind the counter, his head in his hands, weeping softly.

CHAPTER SIX

BURT HAD ALWAYS BEEN uncomfortable around anyone when they cried. It was just a thing with him. Men, women – regardless of their species – crying just made him want to walk away in the other direction.

Which was why Beatrice was the first to move, going straight to the counter.

Burt, on the other hand, hung back with Danny.

"What's going on, Dad?" Danny asked, looking from Colin to the mess on the floor. "Why is Colin crying?"

"I don't know, buddy," Burt said, taking Danny's hand and guiding him to the candy bars and potato chip bags. "I don't know, but your mom will handle it. Why don't we pick this stuff up for Colin."

"But, what about my gum?"

"We'll get your gum, don't you worry, but we have to straighten up here first."

"But, I didn't make this mess. Why do I have to pick it up?" Danny began to get agitated and Burt could sense a meltdown coming on.

"Because, bud, it's the right thing to do. Don't you want to help Colin out?"

"Fine!" Danny yelled, and that was the end of it. Crisis averted. Danny was able to stop his meltdown with that one, solitary word and the two quickly got to work cleaning up the mess around them.

Meanwhile, Beatrice had moved over to Colin's side of the counter and held him, rocking gently back and forth and making soft, soothing, shushing sounds as the pig cried without shame. Burt smiled in a nervous sort of way. The way Colin sounded, Burt thought that if this were a cartoon, great streams of tears would be spraying out of the sides of Colin eyes like small high pressure faucets.

"Colin," Beatrice said. "I can't help you if you don't tell me what happened. Tell me what's wrong, honey."

Colin's crying slowed as he rose from behind the counter.

"A woman came in earlier," Colin began. "The most beautiful woman I'd ever seen. Her hair was like gold. She pretended to like me. Then she stole my car."

"Not your Camaro?" Burt said. "See, Beatrice, I told you that was Colin's car."

"Shush, Burt," said Beatrice. "Go on Colin."

"Well," continued Colin. " She stole my car and then this guy came in looking for her. He had a sword, and a gun. He pointed the gun at me. I've never had a gun pointed at me," tears formed again in Colin's eyes.

"It's okay, Colin," Beatrice said, putting a hand on his shoulder. "He's gone now."

"He asked me where Goldilocks, that's the girl, he asked me where she went, but I was too scared to talk. So he threw candy bars and potato chips at me. But I still wouldn't talk. So then he put his gun away and started being nice to me. So I told him that she took my car and went east, toward your place."

Colin paused and looked at the mess on the floor.

"He said he would clean all this up. But he never did. He just left," Colin began to cry again.

"It's okay, Colin," Beatrice said soothingly, patting Colin's shoulder. "It's okay."

"My car has been stolen, I had a gun in my face, and the store is a mess!" Colin began to shout. "I didn't ask for this! I don't deserve any of this! I'm not even supposed to be here today!" And with that, Colin's eyes rolled up and he dropped to the floor in a dead faint.

CHAPTER
SEVEN

A T THE EXACT MOMENT that Colin Pig had dropped to the floor of the Brick House Gas and Groceries, Jack Horner, the Griswold's head of security, served Goldilocks a cup of coffee in the Griswold House kitchen.

At least, she supposed it was a kitchen. Of course, she knew that it obviously *was* a kitchen, what with all of the ovens and refrigerators and freezers and automated dishwashers. Plus all the counter space filled with mixers and knives and spoons and spices and fruits and vegetables and all the various tools needed to whip up a meal. Then you add to the mix the scores of men and women, both human and animal, all dressed in white uniforms, aprons, and hats. Well, she had to come to the logical conclusion that this was, in fact, a kitchen. She had just never seen a kitchen this size, at least outside of a five-star restaurant.

She sat on a tall stool, practically in the center of the bustling kitchen. Everyone worked with a precision that made her think of the ballet. Every single person in this room, apart from herself and Jack, had a role, and they performed that role with a skill and sense of pride the likes of which hasn't been seen outside of a Peter Jackson trilogy blockbuster movie set.

"I believe that I should contact the authorities," Jack said.

She had to reach deep inside herself for the strength to keep her eyes from rolling in contempt. She'd used the story that she'd been attacked to get inside the house, and now that she was in, she wasn't about to let Johnny Law spoil her chance to get a free meal and possibly a pillow to lay her head.

"Oh please," she said, reaching out and placing a hand on Jack's arm. "I don't want to be any trouble. I just want to forget this whole thing. I just want to rest and wait for my friend."

Then a smell hit her. An aroma that prodded at her senses, took her gently by the hand, pulled her into a loving embrace, caressed her hair with thoughtful affection, and mewled sweet nothings softly into her ear before slapping her across the face with a large open palm. The scent wrapped so completely around her that it nearly pulled her from the stool.

She stood, shaking slightly. She struggled a bit to place her coffee on the stool without spilling or dropping it. Then she stuck her nose high up into the air, and without any thought to how a lady might act in polite society, took one, great, loud and long, sniff.

"Oh my," She said, turning to Jack. "What is that enchanting aroma?"

"That is the chef's famous lobster bisque" said Jack, smiling with pride and pointing to something behind her.

She turned and saw a large man, whom she determined was the head chef based entirely on the sheer immensity of his great floppy white hat. He carefully ladled the lobster bisque into three separate bowls. A great big bowl. A medium sized bowl. And a small child's bowl.

She looked from the three bowls to a small red box on the wall. The box had a glass front, behind which was a red button. Above the red box were the words:

BREAK GLASS IN CASE OF FIRE

She looked from the box back to the three bowls. Then she smiled as the beginnings of a plan began to form in her head.

Her plan was simple, She would just need to distract the army of people in the kitchen long enough to press the fire alarm. The ensuing panic and chaos of the subsequent evacuation would be enough, she hoped, to allow her to slip away, circle back to the kitchen, and feast.

There were, of course, many flaws to her plan. First and foremost, she noticed the sprinklers in the ceiling. Goldilocks wasn't sure how fire sprinklers worked. She was fairly certain they wouldn't just start spitting water when the alarm was pulled, but if they did, it would be like eating in the shower. And from what she understood, the water that comes out of those sprinkler systems is old, filthy, and smelly. No thanks.

Secondly, she wasn't sure what she could do to cause the kind of distraction necessary to draw attention away from her long enough to pull the alarm without anyone realizing that she was the one who had pulled it. She supposed she could start a fire, but a fire would surely get the sprinklers started, and then she would be back to eating in the smelly, filthy shower.

The fact of the matter was, despite the sheer size of the house, which was larger than your average Wal-Mart supercenter, she didn't take into account the amount of people she would have to deal with just to get some food and a place to sleep. Usually, when she broke into a place, the owners were away on vacation and she had the place to herself for a few days. She started to wonder just why she picked this particular house. She'd never tried the whole "home invasion" thing, and while conning a clerk in a convenience store to get you a free burrito was a piece of cake, this job had quickly turned out to be more like a slice of mud pie.

She gave thought to just leaving. Just packing it all in and heading down the road to find an empty place to loot ... but then the smell of lobster bisque took a fantastic voyage throughout her nasal passages, and before she could stop herself, she pointed to the door on the wall opposite of the fire alarm and screamed in mock, yet rather quite convincing, terror.

All heads turned first toward her, then toward the door. This was her chance. She was off like a shot. She crossed the room in little under two seconds, snatched a dish towel from a nearby rack, threw it up over the fire alarm box, and slammed her fist into it, smashing the glass and pushing the fire alarm button at the same time.

The fire alarm sounded throughout the house and a general state of panic and chaos set in as everyone made their way to the nearest exit. The sprinklers did not start spitting forth dirty, stink-water, and for that, she was grateful.

Goldilocks followed the crowd as they exited the kitchen and began to look for a place to duck out when someone grabbed her by the arm.

"You're coming with me." It was Jack Horner. He pulled her from the crowd, down a hallway, and into a room at the end.

The room was small. All that occupied the room were a square wooden table, and two metal folding chairs at either end. Jack pushed her into one chair while he sat in the other, opposite her, glaring at her in anger.

"Just what are you up to?" Jack asked, slamming his hand down on the table.

"I don't know what you're talking about," she said, panic and fear in her voice. "The fire alarm-"

"There is no fire!" Jack interrupted as the alarm continued to sound. "I saw what you did. I saw you push the alarm. What the heck is going on here! What do you want!?"

She sighed, leaned back in her chair, and relaxed.

"Okay," she said. "You want to know what's going on? You want to know who I am and what I'm doing here?"

"You bet your bleached hair I do!"

"Right," she said, leaning forward. "But you probably shouldn't have said that about my hair."

"Wha-", Jack began, but before he could finish, She was on her feet, and she brought her side of the table with her.

As she rose, she tipped the table up on its end and sent it crashing down on Jack. Then she leaped into the air and brought both feet down on the upturned table with Jack beneath it. She began to scream as she jumped up and down on the table, each word coinciding with her landings.

"NEVER! TALK! ABOUT! MY! HAIR!"

She stopped, took a deep breath, and pulled herself together before opening the door and making her way back to the kitchen, leaving Jack, unconscious and alone in the room.

CHAPTER EIGHT

G OLDILOCKS STROLLED INTO THE kitchen like she owned the place, the fire alarm ringing all around her, and went straight to the three bowls of lobster bisque. She went to the largest of the three bowls first, took a spoon, and tried a bit. The bisque burned her tongue and she threw the spoon to the ground in anger as she shouted a curse the likes of which should never be repeated – by anyone – to anyone – for any reason.

It certainly won't be repeated here.

She cursed again when she realized that she just threw her spoon to the ground and in her rage she swept the large bowl of bisque from the counter and smiled in silent satisfaction as it shattered on the floor, spilling lobstery goodness everywhere. She then went looking for another spoon.

Finding a new spoon she skipped the medium sized bowl, fearing it would be just as hot as the large bowl. She figured that the small bowl, having less in it, would have cooled down sooner than the others and went next to that one. Sadly, she was disappointed by how cold the bisque was and so, like its large companion, the small bowl soon found itself in pieces on the floor, its contents mixing with that of its chum.

So she tried the medium sized bowl. She carefully filled her spoon. She brought the spoon to her lips. She took a small, tentative sip. Without warning, her knees went all wobbly and she fell to the floor, landing on her bottom. She smiled as she let the bisque, which was at the perfect temperature, slosh about in her mouth. She moaned. It tasted like nothing she'd ever experienced. It felt like each of her pleasure centers had turned to eleven at the same time.

She began to feel angry and cheated when she realized that she'd just thrown two bowls of this ... perfection, to the ground. What a waste. She wanted to punch something. Instead she swallowed the bisque and was immediately swept away by the sheer ecstasy of the flavors that met in her tummy.

She pulled herself to her feet, spoon in hand, and bent over the bowl once more. She took her time with the bisque. Savoring every drop. Even licking the bowl clean when she could no longer manage to scoop any more on to her spoon.

Once her belly was full, she decided to go exploring. As she moved through the house, she felt the exhaustion of the day settle around her. She wanted a place to just sit for a while. Of course, the continuing high volume claxon of the fire alarm did little to provide an atmosphere of peace and tranquility, but still,

Goldilocks had a talent for putting herself in a completely restful state on command.

After just a few minutes of searching she found a room with three chairs that sat before a fire place on an exquisite Persian carpet. There was a large plump recliner, a medium sized wooden rocking chair, and a small bean bag chair. All three sat in a slight arc facing the fireplace so that the occupants could sit, read, and enjoy the fire.

Silence roared into the room as the fire alarm finally stopped and Goldilocks smiled.

She was about to try out the recliner when she heard the unmistakable sound of a sword being drawn behind her. She turned and found the most attractive man she had ever seen standing just inside the room. It was the Beast. He was holding one of those samurai swords in both hands and he was smiling.

"Hello, Goldilocks," he said.

"Tim," she replied icily.

Then she threw a chair at him.

CHAPTER
NINE

G OLDILOCKS HAS ALWAYS CONSIDERED herself someone who could think quickly on her feet. She's never had a problem assessing a situation and then quickly coming up with a viable solution. She believed it to be one of her greatest assets. She figured it's what has kept her alive during this life of hers, this life of lies and deceit. So while this was the first occasion in which Goldilocks found herself trapped in a strange house with a handsome man who threatened her with a sword, it didn't take her too long to come up with a plan.

The plan, which she decided was actually quite genius, involved the three chairs in front of her. The large recliner, the medium sized wooden rocker, and the small bean bag chair.

She had zero qualms about throwing chairs at people if it meant she lived to steal another day. Besides, the Beast, or Tim (as she knew him), had a sword, and she had jack. So yeah, she felt pretty righteous when it came to throwing chairs at guys with swords.

Unfortunately, she currently found herself standing behind the large, cushy recliner.

"You're looking good," the Beast said, walking slowly toward her. Stalking her. His sword held out before him.

"I'd say the same, but then, you always look good," she replied, backing up and crouching slightly, the back of the recliner behind her. "And of course, you know it."

The Beast just smiled, and with the sudden grace of a jungle cat, he lunged. The Beast was fast. Goldilocks was faster. She leaped into the air, hands over her head, arched backwards, planted both hands on the back of the recliner, and flipped over the top of the chair to land on her hands and feet just as the Beast's sword sliced down into the chair back.

Her first thought upon landing was to throw the recliner at the Beast, but she could see that it was too big, too heavy. There was no way she was getting it off the ground, much less toss it. She raised her hands and cart-wheeled to the left as the Beast pulled his sword free form the chair back, and then brushed the recliner aside as if it was made from papier-mâché.

She was closest to the beanbag chair now, and so she lifted it and threw it at him, knowing that it would do no damage, but then damage wasn't the point, she needed him distracted. The Beast took his attention from her long enough to swat the bean bag away with his free hand. It was only a moment, but a moment was all she needed. She dropped into a low crouch, and using her right hand for balance, swept her left leg out at him. She connected with the backs of his knees and his legs were swept out from under him. The Beast toppled.

Not wasting a second, she was back on her feet. She grabbed the wooden rocking chair and lifted it high above her head. This chair was just right. It was heavy enough to do some serious damage, but not too heavy to lift. She brought it crashing down on his head as he tried to rise. The rocker broke into pieces and he fell back to the floor, unconscious.

"You ain't looking too good now," she said to the still form of the Beast before retreating from the room.

CHAPTER
TEN

T HE BEAST DREAMED.

His mind floated back into his past and danced along memories of days spent with a young woman he knew as Lucy, though most called her something else. Something to do with her hair. His memories were fuzzy. They faded in and out like an old UHF television station on a cloudy day, so he couldn't quite recall.

Goldilocks! That was it. Everyone called her Goldilocks because of her blonde hair. And it did shine like gold, he had to admit that. Of course, it was fake. Her hair was blacker than her heart turned out to be, but she would never admit it.

Goldilocks called him Tim. Which was his name, in a previous life. He no longer used it. He was only the Beast now. He hadn't gone by Tim since before Belle.

Belle. The name tramped across his mind, singing with every step.

Before Lucy there was Belle.

Tim was Tim. Then he was the Beast. Then came Belle. The Beast was gone. He was Tim again. Then Belle left. After, he tried to remain as Tim. Then came Goldilocks. Goldilocks helped. Tim was Tim. But then Goldilocks left. The Beast returned. Now the Beast is all he is.

He rifled through his memories, walking through the storage complex that was his mind and found the room that contained the day that he and Goldilocks had met.

After Belle, Tim went through an elaborate and expensive midlife crisis. He'd bought a hundred thousand dollar red sports car. He'd moved into a trendy loft in the art district of the big city. He'd furnished the loft with top-of-the line furniture and appliances. He'd spent thousands of dollars on the most fashionable clothes. And he danced his nights away in the trendiest clubs, running up monumental bills on drinks alone. Drinks that were not for him. The Beast didn't drink. The drinks were for the ladies.

He had been at one of those clubs the night he had met Goldilocks. He'd bought her a drink. She'd accepted. He'd asked her to dance. They'd danced. They had talked and they had danced. He'd bought drinks and Goldilocks drank them. She'd given him her phone number. Then she'd left.

He had called her the next day, which all of his friends had told him not to do. They'd said that he had to wait at least three days to call. Calling the next day screamed of desperation. But he *was* desperate. She was a drop of water and his life the Sahara. He needed her. And so he'd called. And so they'd dated.

Tim and Goldilocks. Goldilocks and Tim. What a great couple they had made.

Three days later they were in Vegas. They'd married in a ceremony performed by a man dressed as Elvis Presley. Tim had never been happier.

Two days after that, Goldilocks was gone.

All she'd left was a note. She'd said she had to leave, but couldn't explain why. She'd said that she was sorry. She'd said that she loved him; that she'd never meant for any of this to happen. But still, she was gone.

And so Tim went away ... and in his place was the Beast.

The Beast had spent every waking moment since then trying to find Goldilocks. The chase had taken over two years and most of his life savings. But he will never stop. Until his dying breath takes him to the world beyond, the Beast will hunt.

Such is the way of beasts.

CHAPTER ELEVEN

BURT, BEATRICE, AND DANNY Griswold arrived home just in time to hear the fire alarm stop.

The entire household staff milled about on the lawn with a large company of firefighters. The emergency vehicles sat silently in the front yard, their lights spinning and flashing in every direction.

The firefighters stood idly by with nothing to do. Some talked to members of the household staff; the cleaning ladies especially seemed to be getting plenty of attention. Others talked into radios. A few stood off to the side, texting on their cell phones or just sitting in the grass enjoying the day. Henrietta Sugarbaker stalked through the crowd, gnashing her teeth at how everyone was treating her lawn.

"What's going on, Burt?" Beatrice asked. "Was there a fire?"

"I don't know, Bea. I don't see any smoke."

"My Legos!" Danny shouted. He started to run for the house, but Beatrice snatched him back.

Just then, Burt spotted the head of security, Jack, stumbling out the front door. He held his head gingerly as he shuffled along toward them. His nose trickled blood. He looked bad. Like he had had a table slammed on top of him or something.

Burt went to Jack and put a hand on his shoulder.

"What's going on here, Jack? Was there a fire?"

"No sir," Jack said. "No fire."

Jack fell to the grass and landed flat on his bottom.

"Can I get some help here!" Burt shouted to the idle firefighters. "We have an injured man here!"

"No, I'm okay," Jack sputtered. "The girl."

"Girl?" Burt crouched down to Jack's level.

"Goldilocks. The girl. She's still in the house."

"In the house?" Burt scratched at his chin in confusion.

"A girl showed up today after you left. A young woman. She called herself Goldilocks. She said she'd been attacked. I don't know, maybe she was, but something about her felt ... off"

"Go on," Burt said, handing Jack his handkerchief.

"I let her inside and took her to the kitchen to clean up," Jack dabbed at the blood trickling from his nose with the handkerchief. "She refused to allow me to call the authorities. I wanted to sir, you have to believe me."

"It's okay, Jack. Tell me what happened next."

"Mike, the chef, he began to ladle the lobster bisque into your bowls and the girl just went crazy. I think she was hungry. I think the bisque set her off. She started screaming and pointing to the main door to the kitchen. Everyone turned to look at what she was pointing at, but it was nothing. Nothing at all. I turned back to her and she was running like a madwoman toward the opposite wall. She pulled the fire alarm. Everything went berserk after that."

Two paramedics arrived and started poking and prodding at Jack, all the while hemming and hawing and using words that Burt usually heard on popular television shows about doctors who spent more time kissing and taking off their clothes then doing any actual doctoring.

"People were running for the doors," Jack continued. "The girl was screaming. It was a madhouse sir."

"And she's still in there?"

"Yes, sir. I believe she is. And, sir?"

"What is it, Jack?"

"I think that," he paused and swallowed.

Jack looked Burt in the eye and opened his mouth to speak. Burt leaned in. Jack closed his mouth and swallowed again. He opened his mouth once more, only to close it a moment later.

"Good lord, Jack," Burt said. "What is it, man!?"

"I think that she's eating your lobster bisque."

"She's eating my lobster bisque?" Burt turned from Jack and looked out over nothing in particular.

"She's eating my lobster bisque?" Burt said to no one but himself. Then he turned back to Jack.

"She's eating my lobster bisque!" he yelled and anger made its presence known with those words. Burt stood and turned to Beatrice and Danny.

"Burt?" Beatrice could tell something was wrong.

"There's a girl in the house, Bea. She's in there now. She's eating the lobster bisque."

Beatrice straightened, stood tall and firm. Her focus was the house. She looked from the house to Burt. She looked from Burt to the house.

Then she spoke. "Let's go."

CHAPTER TWELVE

T HE BEAST CONTINUED TO dream.

He no longer dreamed of the past, or of memories long forgotten. Instead, his dreams were thick with badgers. Badgers that scampered and danced in hues of blue and green, orange and purple, magenta and taupe. Badgers that bellowed songs in piercing falsetto. Songs of love. Songs of sorrow. Songs of sausages.

At first, he was uncomfortable among the badgers. The myriad of colors made him queasy and their songs made his jaw ache, but soon the badgers fled and he floated along on waves of veal and tripe.

The Beast turned angry. He wasn't one who normally dreamed. At least not this vividly, but here he sat, being pulled along by a river of meat. That cursed woman must have hit him on the head harder than he thought.

The veal and tripe faded to be replaced by nothing. Absolute bleakness.

He simply floated in the void wearing only his boxers. There was no up. No down. No forwards nor backwards. No sense of anything at all. The Beast, who was not one to give into fear, suddenly found himself overwhelmed with a sense of terror so complete that he discovered himself wrapped in it like a caterpillar in a chrysalis. The Beast became fear, and he didn't like it. Not one bit. He was alone in the emptiness.

The Beast wept.

Then something caught his eye. A glint of pale yellow in the distance. It flickered slightly, this tiny dot of yellow, and he felt comfort in it. He yearned to be near the yellow, to embrace it, to let it fill his heart and his soul. He needed the yellow. But how to escape the void? How to leave the emptiness? The Beast found that if he directed his thoughts *toward* the small swatch of color, that the yellow grew closer. So that was just what he did.

As he neared the yellow, it grew from a small patch in the distance to a great swatch of yellow blobs, a field of blurry objects the color of gold that began to fill all that he could see. He directed a sense of urgency into his thoughts and the yellow grew swiftly closer, the forms becoming more distinct as they came into focus. It was a great valley of golden roses which stretched forth into oblivion. Tears formed in his eyes as he realized that he could smell the scent that roiled forth from the field of flowers. They smelled of stale cigarettes and alcohol. It was an aroma most would find distasteful, but the Beast found divine.

Without warning his progression toward the valley simply halted. He hung motionless in the void. Before him was the valley of yellow. A forest of dark, barren, dead trees suddenly sprang up between himself and the yellow. The Beast stepped into the trees and found himself fully clothed and with his sword and gun. The clothing and weapons brought him little comfort as the dead trees began to sway back and forth in a wind that was not there.

The trees seemed to crowd in around him the way regulars at a neighborhood pub gathered round outsiders and he rested a hand on the revolver at his side, taking comfort in the feel of the grip. He could no longer see the yellow field, but he could still sense it out there, somewhere beyond the dark wood.

A path opened up between the trees. A path paved of millions upon millions of small flowers, the same color of yellow as the roses he could no longer see. He stepped onto the path knowing that it would take him to the field of yellow roses. The path would take him home. He stepped swiftly.

He walked for hours, the scenery around him remained unchanged, yet still he continued his trek. The hours turned into days, though the sun never set, a sun that he had not even realized was there until the heat began to beat down upon him, weighing him down, fighting him, trying to keep him from his goal.

The Yellow.

Yet he never faltered. He strode forward with grim determination, his mind set and his spirits high, knowing that the Yellow was there, just beyond the wood. So his journey continued until at last he could see the end of the forest. He could see the field of yellow roses, and his walk turned into a run.

A joy filled him. A joy like he had never known. The feeling grew as he ran and he opened himself up to it. Swam in it. Let it become him.

Just then, a roar erupted from within the trees, stopping him in his tracks. A roar of such magnitude that it seemed to encompass everything. The trees around him shook with the force; leaves and small bits of dead bark fell to the ground. He gripped his head and bent forward from the pain. Even the fillings in his teeth vibrated as the bestial cry continued.

Then there was silence, a silence so complete that it simply exploded into being around him. He felt disorientated as the silence fled as quickly as it appeared and the sound of creaking wood and snapping branches came to him. Something large moved through the trees. Moving toward him. He pulled the revolver as sweat broke out on his brow.

It emerged from the trees on all fours and loped out onto the path, standing between him and the field of yellow roses. It was an immense shaggy creature of brown fur. It was a bear. But a bear of such size and power that even the trees appeared to shrink back from it. It stood on its hind legs and let out another thunderous roar that shook the very earth beneath the his feet.

The Beast took an involuntary step back. An anger radiated from the bear. A hostility so thick that he felt he could freeze it on a stick and sell it to evil little children. The bear wanted him dead. He knew that for sure and for certain, but he had to get to those roses, needed to get to the roses. He felt that in every square inch of his being. He knew, just somehow knew, that if he could get to that field he would no longer have to be the Beast. He would only need to be Tim. But the bear, the bear that radiated with hatred and rage at his very presence, stood in his path. The bear wasn't giving an inch, allowing him to go no further. So the Beast did what came natural and emptied all the revolver into the bear.

The bear dropped back down to all fours and looked at him for a moment, cocking its massive head to the side in a quizzical manner that looked almost human. That's when the bear smiled. Actually smiled.

"Oh come now," the bear said, its voice like molasses running down the inside of a bass drum. "I'm sure you can do much better than that." And with that said, the bear charged.

CHAPTER THIRTEEN

COLIN PIG SAT ONCE more behind the counter at the Brick House Gas and Groceries, reading a comic book, and waiting patiently for his shift to be up so that he could finally go home and wallow in his misery. The first thing Colin had done after that woman had driven off in his car was to call the Grimmelton Police Department to report that his baby had been stolen. Immediately after that, he called his two brothers, Larry and Gary, and gave them the news about his Camaro. They didn't seem to care. He'd also asked if one of them would come take the rest of his shift so that he could go home. Their answer came as a resounding "no".

After he had passed out, right in front of the Griswold family, he found that Beatrice Griswold had stayed beside him until he had come around. Once he was coherent again, Beatrice insisted that Colin call the Police once more to report the man who had threatened to shoot Colin in the face. He hadn't actually said that he would, in fact, shoot Colin in the face, but a gun barrel speaks louder than the person holding the gun, and Colin felt fairly certain that he understood exactly what that gun barrel had been saying. Beatrice also insisted that he call his brothers again and explain that this life threatening incident had come to fray upon Colin's nerves and request again that they let him go home early. Once again the answer he received from his brothers amounted to a simple, yet clear and resounding "no". Once his calls were made, and the Griswolds were on their way back home, Colin grabbed a soda out of the cooler and a comic off the spinner rack and settled in for the afternoon lag.

There wasn't a lot for him left to do at that point. The Griswold's had cleaned the store pretty well before they left, which meant that all Colin had to look forward to was the wait. So Colin waited. He waited for the Police because he needed to make a statement regarding his stolen car as well as give them a description of the man with the gun. Then he would wait for his shift to end so that he could go home, take a Tylenol PM, and sleep till tomorrow morning.

Colin idly flipped through the pages of the comic on his counter when an electronic bell sounded, signifying that a customer had just walked in through the double glass doors.

"Welcome to the Brick House Gas and Groceries. May I help you?" Colin said in the purest of monotone without looking up from the comic.

The customer, whomever they were, walked right up to the counter before speaking. "Why thank you, son," he said, sounding like a real Southern gentleman. "I do hope you can. You see, I'm looking for my wife. Maybe you've seen her."

"I see lots a people," Colin said, again without looking up. "She got a name?"

"Why yes, she surely does. Most folks call her Goldilocks."

At the sound of the name, that hated name, the name that he now associated with misery and fear, everything within him froze. This turned out to be somewhat of a blessing, otherwise he may have made himself a little mess right there behind the counter. It just wasn't turning out to be his day.

Colin's eyes rose slowly from over the top of the comic and they goggled at the sight of the man that stood at his counter. Colin's mouth gaped as he took the stranger in. The man who stood before him must have recently stepped off the set of a Western, or maybe out of time, for he dressed like a historical resident of Dodge City, Kansas or Tombstone, Arizona. In fact, Colin thought the man would look right at home standing next to Billy the Kid, Jesse James, or Wyatt Earp. His clothes were city clothes, not the sort your average cowpoke would don for a long cattle drive. No, this was no cowboy, this guy had the look of a professional gambler and gunfighter. His hat, coat, pants, and string tie were black. His shirt was white. He wore a revolver at his left hip, the grip sticking out forwards so that the man would have to reach across his body with his right hand to pull it. He had another revolver sticking out of his coat in a shoulder holster under his right arm. The guns looked well used. The man wore a long, yet meticulously trimmed mustache. He was rather thin, and somewhat frail, yet he radiated a sense of something dangerous. Like a snake – coiled and ready to strike at a moment's notice –

yet he also maintained a look of comfort, ease, and complete self-assurance. But it was more than that. The man in black looked at Colin the way most people looked at a bug. Colin felt true fear for the first time in his life and he realized what it was about the man in black that troubled him so. His eyes, they were dark, almost black, even beyond the iris and the pupils. The man was evil, pure and simple. Colin could feel it rolling off of the man in waves.

"What's the matter son, cat got your tongue?" The stranger said, smiling up at Colin.

"Goldilocks?"

"That's what she goes by. Look here son, I don't believe that I got your name."

"Colin."

"Colin, you can call me Doc. Would you like to help me, Colin?"

"Yes," Colin said, almost involuntarily.

"See, I knew you would. I just knew you would. Here's the thing Colin," Doc took a step back and looked around the store. "I know that you know what I need to know."

"What?"

"Pay attention, son. I'm going to make it real easy for you." Doc completed his quick look around the store, stepped up to Colin, pulled a long knife out from under the back of his coat, and lay it atop the counter.

Colin looked from the knife to Doc, then back to the knife. He looked up and saw something in the man's eyes. Something dark and twisted. For a moment, those eyes showed Colin an image of what Doc would do to the pig with the knife he had placed between them, and so he went ahead and had himself a little accident there behind the counter.

Doc smiled again. But the smile was not kindly, nor reassuring. He looked more like a wolf showing its teeth. "You're going to tell me where she went. Heck, son, you don't even have to tell me, you just have to point out the direction. You do that for me, and I won't have to do anything nasty to you. I'm sure you don't want me to do anything nasty to you. Ain't that right, son?"

"Yes," Colin said with the barest hint of a whisper. Then Colin pointed in the direction that Goldilocks went, his finger shaking so violently that the trembling soon infested his entire body.

"Thank you, son. That was right kindly of you." Doc put the knife away and started to turn from the counter when the electronic bell over the door sounded again.

Colin and Doc both turned to look at the double glass doors and found a Grimmelton City Police Officer standing there looking back and forth between the two of them.

"Everything okay here, Colin?" the officer asked.

"It was," Doc said, and in a blur of motion, pulled both pistols and opened fire.

CHAPTER FOURTEEN

EVER SINCE CARL FRIENDLY had been a little boy, all he wanted to be was a Grimmelton City Police Officer. His dad was a Grimmelton City Police Officer. His grandpa was a retired Grimmelton City Police Officer. Each and every male Friendly, stretching back to Roy Friendly, Grimmelton's first city marshal, had been an officer of the law.

They still considered him a rookie on the force, having only served for ten months, and he had had the good fortune, or misfortune as it may be, to get the call regarding an incident at the Brick House Gas and Groceries. The report hadn't been too clear, something about a man waving a gun around and the theft of a car, but that's really all one needed when they were a sworn officer of the law. So he got into his police cruiser, and drove over to the store.

When he arrived, he noticed that there were no cars in the lot, or at the pumps, but he could see a man at the counter talking to Colin. A man in a hat. A man in black. Carl sat in his cruiser and watched the man through the window of the store. Carl watched Colin too. Colin seemed scared. The man in black pulled something out from under the back of his coat and put it on the counter. He couldn't see what it was, but he didn't like it.

Carl picked up his radio. "Car 42 to base. Car 42 to base. Over."

"This is base, Car 42. What is your situation? Over."

"Base, I'm sitting here outside the Brick House Gas and Groceries and I'm spying what appears to be an unfriendly situation. I can't confirm, but Colin's looking a bit stressed. Over."

"Roger, Carl. I'll send a couple of other units your way. Over."

"Thanks, Jen. Over and out."

He stepped out of the cruiser. He adjusted the mirrored sunglasses he wore and unbuttoned the protective flap that covered his sidearm. He walked slowly toward the store, keeping an eye on Colin and the man in black.

Upon reaching the double glass doors, he stepped to the side, avoiding the pressure plate that would cause the doors to slide open automatically. Instead he stood still and tried to hear what the two inside were saying. But before he could make out any of the words, the man in black picked up the object he had set on the counter earlier. From here, he could make it out quite clearly. A knife, and a tooting big one at that. Without another thought, he stepped onto the pressure plate, watched the doors slide open, and walked inside.

"Everything okay here, Colin?" he asked, never taking his eyes off the man in black.

"It was," the man in black said.

The man in black smiled, his hands blurred, and then there were two back to back explosions. Something punched him in the chest, twice, knocking all the air out him and slamming him backwards through the open doorway of the store. He landed flat on his back as the sound of a police siren, followed by screeching tires, sounded behind him. A car door slammed.

"Freeze!" someone shouted from behind him. "Drop 'em, pal! Drop 'em!"

Gunfire erupted from both behind and in front of him. He could feel the bullets as they flew over him. He instinctively curled himself into the fetal position, his arms over his head, as shot after shot zipped over him. More sirens could be heard in the distance. They grew closer as more tires screeched into the lot behind him.

His chest felt like it was on fire. He felt around with his hands but found no blood. His vest wasn't pierced, then. All officers were required to wear Kevlar vests before going out on patrol. Most officers didn't like to wear them. They are uncomfortable and hold in your body heat, making you sweat. But today proved to Carl why they are so very important.

He flipped over onto his stomach as Armageddon erupted all around him. He crawled out from the line of fire and made it back to his car. He took cover behind the front tire, the car between him and the store, and took in the scene before him.

On his side of the lot were four of the town's police cruisers. Each with two officers. Five officers appeared to be down. The other three fired their weapons at the man in black.

The man in black? He still stood in the doorway of the store. He didn't seek cover. He just squeezed off shot after shot. Bullets zinging by and landing all around him. Yet the man in black remained calm. As a matter of fact, he laughed as he fired. And his guns? His guns looked like the kind of revolvers a gunfighter from the Old West would use. And yet, he never stopped to reload. He counted twelve, thirteen, fourteen, fifteen shots. They never stopped. They just kept coming, and for some reason, he felt that the man in black was just toying with them. He could sense that so far the man in black had hit everything he had aimed at, and luckily enough for Carl and his fellow officers, the man in black had aimed at everything but them. Otherwise, he thought, they would all be dead.

He ducked back down behind his car as a bullet popped into the hood just inches from his face.

And just like that, it stopped.

The sounds of the shots echoing out into the distance and the heavy breathing of the surviving officers as they gulped for air were all he could hear. Taking a chance, he took a quick look over the hood of the car and found the doors to the store closed.

Just then one of the speakers over the pumps crackled on and a voice came out of them. The voice, he could only assume, of the man in black.

"Gentleman," the man in black said, "I want to make this as easy as possible on everyone involved. Know that if I wished for your death, then you would all be dead. It's really just that simple."

Carl believed him.

"I'm only going to say this once," the man in black continued. "So pay attention and take heed. I will kill this little pig here if you all don't get back into your cars, leave this place, and go back to your tiny little lives. I will place the barrel of my pistol against young Colin's head and squeeze the trigger, thus removing him from this equation, and from existence."

Carl exchanged nervous glances with the men and women around him.

"Furthermore," said the man in black. "I will come out of this shabby little building and end each and every life out there I see with a badge pinned to its chest. I hope I've made myself clear. You have ten seconds to comply."

Carl looked to the remaining officers, looking for guidance. The other officers looked just as confused and unsure as he felt. There was nothing now but the silence, which did not last long. Colin's voice replaced that of the man in black through the speakers at the pumps. It was a voice of fear and panic.

"Help me."

CHAPTER FIFTEEN

A FTER LEAVING THE BEAST unconscious and alone in the room with three chairs, Goldilocks set out to find a place to rest. She often found herself exhausted after a big meal and a bit of violence. She figured that Tim, as she knew the Beast, would be out for an hour at least, so if she could just find a bed, she could possibly get herself a twenty minute power nap. The only problem, of course, were the multitudes of people currently hanging about on the front lawn.

Now that the fire alarm was no longer ringing, she supposed that those folks would probably want to eventually come back into the house. Most people, when put in the same situation, would try to find the nearest exit and leave this place in the dust, but she wasn't most people – which, of course, most people would find a little dumb and not daring in the way she thought of herself.

She made her way up to the second floor, moving quickly and quietly. She walked past a large window that looked out over the front lawn and for the first time got a good look at the upheaval she had caused in the lives of the people who lived here.

No less than four red fire engines, all with lights flashing and rotating, sat on the lawn in no discernible pattern. They were all parked in such a way that told anyone looking that the fire department was on the scene and everyone else was invited to come and watch. Along with the fire engines, she saw three police cars, one ambulance, and a small pizza delivery truck. The firefighters, now that the alarm had stopped ringing and there was no obvious risk of fire, were all sitting around out on the lawn eating pizza.

Goldilocks decided that, considering the circumstances, maybe the whole 'taking a nap' thing probably wasn't the brightest idea she'd ever had and figured that it was best to get out while the getting was good. So she did what she did best. She fled.

After many twists and turns, she found herself looking down from the top of the main staircase. As she descended she could see that the staircase ended at the front door to the house, which wouldn't have been such a big deal if it wasn't opening at that very moment.

Goldilocks, nearly to the bottom, froze on the steps as three bears walked into the house through the open front door. In first was the male, a large, well ... *huge*, brown bear, possibly a grizzly. He was dressed casually in a pair of khaki pants and a green polo shirt. Behind him came a slightly smaller, but still quite large, female wearing a flower print sundress and wide brimmed, woven, sun hat. Lastly came the cub. The cub, which looked about as tall as Goldilocks, wore a red cap, jeans, and a plain white t-shirt.

The large male spotted her first, pointed up at her and growled, "You don't belong here."

"Um," was about the only response she could come up with as she started to back up the stairs.

"What are you doing here?" The female asked.

"Well," she said in return.

"Who are you?" The big male asked.

"Uh," she said as she continued backwards up the stairs.

Suddenly, the big male stepped up onto the first stair and said in a loud authoritative voice, "Freeze!"

She stopped moving. She was a statue. A solidified object perched with one foot on the last step and one on the landing just above. She couldn't help herself. The bear's voice was so persuasive, so commanding that she had no choice but to obey. Sweat broke out on every surface of her body that contained sweat glands, and even a few that didn't.

The big male moved slowly toward her. His hands – Paws? – on either side of the staircase, clutching the railing as he ascended.

He stopped about six stairs from her so that he could look her in the eye. "What's your name?" he asked.

"Goldilocks," she said as the sweat began to rain from her brow.

"Why are you in my house?"

"I, um … I, well." She couldn't say it.

"You told Jack that you'd been attacked."

"I did?"

"Yes, you did. Why are you in my house?" the bear asked again.

"I was hungry."

"You were hungry."

"I was hungry."

"So instead of asking for a little help, a little charity, you conned your way into my house and stole my food."

"Um," she tried to swallow but her mouth was dry. Evidently all the moisture in her body had been converted into sweat.

"You assaulted Jack."

"Uh."

"You stole my food."

"Uh."

"You lied."

Goldilocks ran out of clever responses.

"You brought violence and deceit into my house. MY HOUSE!" He roared out the last two words.

Goldilocks, being human, did what any would do when being yelled at by a bear the size of, well ... a bear.

She screamed.

And then she fainted.

CHAPTER SIXTEEN

O FFICER CARL FRIENDLY WAS overwhelmed by a deep sense of desperation. He had to do something. Colin was all alone with the man in black and if he didn't do something in ten seconds, Colin may very well die.

Carl exchanged glances with the officers around him. They all looked just as uncertain as he did. Finally, he just couldn't take it anymore.

"This is crap," he said, checking his gun, a Glock 21. He pulled the magazine and made sure he was fully loaded. He was. He slammed the magazine into place and pulled back the slide. "That guy's gonna kill Colin if we don't do something."

"He's going to kill Colin if we *do* do something!" Gilbert Hines said.

"Not if we handle this right."

"What do you suggest?"

"Cover me," Carl holstered his pistol, snapping the safety strap down over the top of it and stepped out from behind his cruiser. He raised his hands into the air and called out, "I want to talk!"

His only response was silence.

"Let Colin go! Take me instead!"

More silence.

Carl just stood there, hands in the air, feeling like an idiot, waiting, unsure of what to do next.

That was when Carl got his response. The silence was broken by the sound of a gunshot from within the store.

Carl jumped at the sound and stared in open-mouthed shock. *He did it*, he thought. *The bastard shot Colin.* He scrambled back behind his cruiser, pulled his pistol and aimed it at the store when the speaker crackled.

"I warned you," the man in black said over the cheap, funnel-shaped speakers. "You can't say I didn't warn you. The pig's death is on your hands, not mine."

Carl had never known rage before, not like the rage he felt now. He hadn't really known Colin that well. He'd only known him as the pig from the store. The pig that sold him coffee each morning. The pig that Carl would never see again. Regardless, Colin was a life. An innocent life that some stranger just took. Stolen right out of the world. A life taken with no more thought than it takes to step on an ant. Carl had devoted his entire self to helping people. Defending the innocent. Protecting those who could not protect themselves. And today, here in this parking lot, he had failed. That's not something that he was willing to accept.

Carl opened fire. Aiming each shot so that they went through the window behind the counter, on the other side should be the man in black. His fellow officers followed suit and the window shattered. Carl and the other officers stopped and started to reload when the double glass doors slid open.

The man in black stepped out holding a revolver in each hand.

The rest was somewhat of a blur. The man in black opened fire, and Carl recalled that actual flames erupted from each gun, as if the bullets themselves burned. Like tracer bullets, yet not. To him it looked like the guns were firing the very flames of Hell itself.

The officers around him broke and ran. He remained where he was until he'd emptied his gun at the man in black. Then he too ran. The way he figured it, you can't go around shooting off guns that emit the very flames of Hell itself around an island of gas pumps without risk of something going up in a violent explosion. So yes, he ran for his life.

Then came the explosion and he was pushed off of his feet. It was like a giant hand had reached out and swatted him into the street like he was made of straw. He rolled about a bit before coming to rest against the far curb and he thought it might be a good idea to just lie there and bleed for the time being. It seemed like the right thing to do, anyway. His body was one giant pain center. As he lay there, he thought that there might be a spot on the back of his left knee, about the size of a dime, that didn't hurt, but the rest of him was in agony. The world became blurry and indistinct. His thoughts became difficult to grasp, like holding water in a pair of fishnet stockings. He may have even passed out for a time but he couldn't be sure.

After a few moments the world started to clear and Carl began to move, taking it in easy, small steps. He wiggled the toes on his right foot, then his left. They moved with little pain. He rotated both ankles. Everything had gone swimmingly thus far. He arched each knee. So far so good. He wiggled his fingers, rotated his wrists, bent his elbows, and lifted his arms. He hadn't passed out yet, so his outlook was bright. But now came the real test.

Carl sat up, slowly. It took him a few moments but he got there. He looked around. He could see nothing but smoke and fire, so he pulled himself to his feet. His vision began to blur and his stomach contents threatened to come out and play, but he fought it and remained upright. His cruiser was gone, so were the others, except for one. Gilbert had parked his cruiser closer to the road. It lay on its side, but it was intact.

The store, the Brick House Gas and Groceries, was gone. It was just no longer there. There was nothing but a streak of black ash where the building once stood. No frame, no glass, no water pipes spraying water into the air, no wires spitting sparks. Nothing at all. And that meant, no Colin.

Carl stood dazed as he contemplated what had just happened. A stranger, guns that shot fire, and Colin dead. Plus, the Brick House was just gone. That doesn't happen from a simple gas explosion. Yet, there it was – or wasn't, as the case may be. What was he dealing with here?

Carl checked his belt, he still had his gun and a few spare magazines, but he needed more. He needed a lot more. He made his way over to Gilbert's cruiser. The car lay on its passenger side, and the driver's side window was down. He leaned in and retrieved the shotgun from its cradle on the dashboard. Then, using the lever on the console, popped the trunk. In the trunk was a large, black duffel bag. He pulled it out, set it on the ground, knelt, and unzipped it. Inside were three boxes of shells for the shotgun, twelve spare (and fully loaded) magazines for a Glock 21 (the standard issue side arm for the entire department), and a half dozen flash bangs – grenades designed to stun and disorient.

Carl loaded the guns, zipped up the duffel, and stood. He shouldered the duffel, holstered his pistol, and holding the shotgun Carl realized that he had no idea where the man in black went.

Just then, from up the road, over by Griswold House at the top of the hill, the sound of gunfire erupted, lasting for nearly two minutes.

Officer Carl Friendly, ignoring all involuntary human instincts to avoid danger whenever possible, walked toward the sound of the gunfire, and possibly, the man in black.

CHAPTER SEVENTEEN

O NCE UPON A TIME, before a man dressed in black destroyed the Brick House Gas and Groceries, before a Pig named Colin had given a burrito to a woman who had stolen his car, and before a small bear named Danny did a dance on his front lawn for shooting his dad with a suction cup dart, there lived a beautiful young woman named Lucy Goodnight.

Lucy Goodnight was a bright, warm, caring, and selfless girl who had always strived to be the best she could be. She had been at the top of her class in high school, helped little old ladies cross the street, and volunteered at her local animal shelter.

Then one day, Lucy met a man, an older man, and fell in love. His name was John, but everyone called him Doc, and so did she.

They soon married and Lucy could not imagine a life with more happiness. He was a kind man. Loving, dependable, honorable, and forthright. Everything she looked for, everything she desired. He was also fabulously wealthy, cultured, and refined, but Lucy didn't care about the money. She didn't care about the big house, the fancy car, the stables, the expensive clothes, and jewelry. She cared about her man, and he cared about her. That's all Lucy needed.

Unfortunately for Lucy, it was all a lie.

The marriage was about control, not love. It was about her husband's desire to have a beautiful young woman on his arm, a beautiful young woman he could show off and dominate. She was just another possession to him. Something that other men desired, but only *he* could attain. He was cruel to Lucy. He punished her for the smallest of transgressions. He would lock her in a small closet for the night if she neglected to laugh at one of his jokes during a dinner party. If she dared to interrupt him while he spoke, he would make her sleep outside in the rain, with nothing but the clothes she had on for shelter. He was not the man she thought he was. So she got out.

It was one of those nights he had made her sleep outside on the back lawn. She had to sleep on the grass. No shelter. No pillow. No blanket. Just the clothes on her back. It took nearly three hours of restlessness, lying there in the grass, before she had finally realized a hard truth. Nothing kept her there. Nothing could stop her from just getting up and walking away. Nothing at all. Doc was asleep, he had no one watching her, no wall nor gate barred her way, she could just simply ... walk away.

It hurt her to understand that she was in a prison of her own making. She had made the walls, the lock, the cell. Doc didn't need to watch her, didn't need to lock her in, he was confident that she wouldn't leave because she was told not to. It was that simple. She would stay because Doc had told her to stay. And with that her hurt turned to anger. The anger made her brave. So she got up from the grass she had been sleeping on, brushed herself off, and walked away.

She still had her purse on her, so she walked to the closest ATM and took out as much money as was allowed, which was more than the average limit. Doc owned the bank, so he got considerations that others simply did not.

With cash in hand she walked to the bus station and bought a ticket for whichever bus left soonest. She slept soundly on the bus as it trundled along the dark highway. It had been easier than she expected. She was out, and she had managed to stay out for years.

Not legally. Technically, in the eyes of the law, she was still married to the man ... the monster. She understood that running was the only way out. Her husband would not allow a divorce. People didn't leave him. It just didn't happen. She knew that had she gone that route, had she perused the legal option, she would now be dead. So she got out the only way she knew how. She ran.

She'd bleached her hair, changed her look, and changed her entire lifestyle. She went from fashionably bland and refined to trendy and flashy. She went from jet black to blonde. She hit the clubs. She wore the clothes. Once she was honest, forthright, and honorable. Now she lied, cheated, and stole. She changed her entire persona to escape, to stay away, to keep from being found. Once, she was the shy and bookish Lucy Goodnight. Now she was Goldilocks. She had become someone else entirely, the opposite of Lucy Goodnight. She knew that Lucy wouldn't like Goldilocks. But she didn't have a choice if she wanted to stay alive.

Goldilocks was a materialistic club girl who wouldn't think twice about stealing a man's wallet while she stole his heart. She trashed public restrooms, wore tasteless and revealing clothing, and keyed expensive cars whenever the mood struck.

Goldilocks lived the good life, using her looks and her lies to go from place to place, getting what she needed, and staying hidden in plain sight. It turned out to be quite easy, provided that she not stay in one place too long.

But then she got stupid. She got comfortable. She met a man and everything changed. This man wasn't like the others. He made her want to be better. Better than Goldilocks. He made her want to be Lucy again. He could see Lucy through Goldilocks, and it was Lucy he fell in love with, though Goldilocks was how he knew her. She couldn't help herself. She got close to the guy. Allowed him in. She didn't tell him the truth about herself, but she would have, if it hadn't have been for the rat, she would have told him everything.

She'd been running for just over three years. She thought she was safe. So she stopped running and settled down into her new life with her new man. All was good again. All was as it should be. But good things never last. She was over two thousand miles away, on the other side of the county, but still her husband found her. All because she broke her own rule. She stayed put.

Goldilocks was at the mall, shopping for the kind of jeans that are made to look old and worn out, though they were new. She found the jeans she wanted in a store called Trendy Trends. Making her way to the front register, jeans in hand, she froze when she saw one of her husband's goons. He was a real rat. Actually, he was in fact, a genuine rat. He was just over a foot tall and wore a cheap suit. Furthermore, she recognized this rat. His name was

Phil. He was in charge of retail operations for one of her husband's companies here on the East Coast. He walked along the concourse of the mall, just outside Trendy Trends. He hadn't spotted her yet, he was too busy doing what everyone else around him was doing; walking with his head down, looking into his phone, and texting. If she was lucky enough, he wouldn't see her at all.

Goldilocks put the jeans back on the rack and slowly backed away. She turned and walked to the back of the store and went right for the dressing rooms. She just had a hand on a handle to one of the dressing room doors when she heard the voice behind her.

"Excuse me, young lady. You work here?"

"No, no I don't," Goldilocks said, keeping her back to him. She recognized Phil's high pitched voice.

"Hey, you know it ain't polite to talk to someone without looking at 'em. Turn around there, let's get us a good look at you."

Goldilocks didn't reply.

"Aw, come on now. I like what I'm seeing from here," at a foot tall Phil would have a great view of her rear end, "but let's see if the front is as good as the back."

"Come on, mister, I just want to buy some jeans," said Goldilocks, staying where she was.

"Is there a problem here?" A woman in a Trendy Trends smock said, walking up to Goldilocks.

"Yes," said Goldilocks. "This rat is bothering me."

The woman looked from Goldilocks to Phil, and Goldilocks saw a mixture of recognition and fear.

"Good morning, Giselle," came Phil's voice behind Goldilocks.

"Mr. Jenner, what a pleasant surprise." Giselle didn't look pleased.

"I need to go over this month's books, Giselle."

"Of course, sir, whatever you need."

Goldilocks tried to use the opportunity to slip away. She turned and ran right into the chest of a man in a suit that looked even cheaper than Phil's. A man that was built like the Great Wall of China, thick and wide.

"Where you off to there, sweets?" Phil said as the Great Wall took her by the arm.

Phil walked around her and looked up into her face. "Well now, you are a pretty one, aren't you." And then a look of recognition sparked in his eyes. "Lucy? Lucy Goodnight? Is it really you?" He smiled, and if you've ever seen a rat smile, you'll know it's not a pleasant thing to see. "I don't believe it, it is you. Where you been, Luce? Everybody's been looking for ya."

"Phil. You didn't see me."

"Hey, whatchoo saying there, Luce? You know I see you. You see me seeing you. Why you gotta say I ain't seeing you?"

Goldilocks sighed and said, "Come on, Phil. Just keep this between us, okay. He can't know."

"Oh, he's gonna know this, toots. Ain't no way he ain't gonna know this. He's paying big money to anyone who can tell him where you are. You broke his heart, little girl. What did you expect would happen?"

"Come on, Phil. We're friends, right? At least we used to be, sort of."

"Yeah, we friends. But I ain't stupid. I ain't gonna cross him. I like life a little too much. Sorry, Luce."

Phil pulled a tiny cell phone from an inside jacket pocket, flipped it open, and began to dial. Goldilocks panicked. She tried to pull herself from the Great Wall's grip, but she might as well have had her hand in a forty ton block of cement.

Goldilocks looked to Giselle. Their eyes met. Goldilocks could see in Giselle's eyes that she wanted to help, and she would have, but she couldn't. Like Phil, Giselle liked life a little too much as well.

So Goldilocks kicked Phil. Kicked him like she was a professional field goal kicker for a big name NFL team and the rat was the football. Phil, she noticed with amusement, was about the size of a football. He dropped his phone as he sailed through the air. There was a wet sound as he smacked against the wall of the store. His body hung there for a moment, stuck to the wall. Then, with a little pop, it fell back and landed with a thud on the carpeted floor.

Giselle screamed. The Great Wall was so stunned that for a moment, he loosened his grip. A moment was all Goldilocks needed. She swiveled and gave the Great Wall a kick in his special place. He let go of her arm and crumpled.

Goldilocks ran. She didn't go home. She didn't call the new guy in her life. She just dropped her phone in a nearby trashcan, hailed a cab, and told the driver to take her to the airport. An hour later she was on a Boeing 717 and on her way to the heartland.

She didn't have a destination in mind. She just had to keep moving. No more stopping. No more staying put. She had learned her lesson. Her life would be always on the run until she died, or he did. But knowing her husband the way she did, that wouldn't be happening anytime in the next few thousand years.

CHAPTER EIGHTEEN

WELL, I SURE HOPE you're proud of yourself, Burt," Beatrice said, coming up the stairs and kneeling down to take the girl's hand in her own. "You've frightened this poor girl half to death."

"She's the one that defiled the sanctity of our home, Bea," Burt said in a growl.

"Yes, yes, but look at her, Burt. She's just a girl."

"You were just as angry as me, Bea," Burt said.

"I know. I know I was. But that was until you bullied the poor thing into catatonia."

Burt sighed heavily and tried to calm down. He was having a hard time of it. He wasn't like his wife. She was quick to forgive. To forget. To get on with things and get the job done. Burt, on the other hand, had trouble letting things go. Burt could hold on to an insult or a slight like a starving rat held on to cheese. Burt stored away each and every little offense and could recall them like a computer, even after everyone else involved had forgotten all about it. Back in grade school, second grade, Fredric Bollington had stolen Burt's lunch from his desk and ate it. Actually, it turned out that Fredric had just gotten confused and took Burt's lunch by accident. The two did have the exact same A-Team lunch box after all, and the two did sit right next each other. So Burt could understand how Fredric could have made the mistake. But to this day, Burt still holds a grudge. He doesn't really have a choice. It's how he's wired.

"Well, what do you think we should do, Bea?" Burt said.

"Is the lady dead?" Danny asked, coming up the steps and peaking around Burt at Goldilocks.

"No, bud," Burt said. "She's just sleeping.

"I want some gum," Danny said.

Beatrice handed Burt her purse and said, "Danny's gum is in my purse."

Burt gave Danny some gum and the two stood off to the side as Beatrice tried to get Goldilocks to wake up.

"Go get the girl some water, Burt," Beatrice said.

And so, grumbling to himself the entire way to the kitchen and back, Burt got Goldilocks a glass of water. By the time he got back, Goldilocks had come to.

"There, there," Beatrice was saying, helping Goldilocks sit up. "You're going to be okay."

Burt handed the glass of water to Beatrice, who then handed it over to Goldilocks. Goldilocks drank slowly and looked around, her eyes bulging with terror when they met Burt's. Burt looked over at Beatrice who was looking back at him with a stern expression. Burt looked back to Goldilocks.

"Look," Burt began, looking down and rubbing the back of his neck. "I'm sorry I frightened you, young lady." He looked back at Beatrice. Her gazed had softened a bit.

"No," Goldilocks said. "I'm the one who's sorry. I never should have come into your home this way. It's just," Goldilocks stopped and looked down.

"What's wrong, dear?" Beatrice asked, holding the girl's hand.

Goldilocks was silent. She thought back over her life. All the choices she's made. All the people she's hurt. Her failed marriage. The one true light in her life and how she left it behind. She couldn't continue living this way anymore. But she'd been on the run now for so long that she wasn't sure if she knew any other way.

Beatrice looked from Goldilocks to Burt. Burt looked from Beatrice to Goldilocks. Danny chewed his gum and looked to all three. Danny then walked over to Goldilocks, knelt down beside her and gave her the one thing in the world she just happened to need right at that very moment.

Danny gave Goldilocks a hug.

◆　◆　◆　◆　◆

Goldilocks burst into tears and clung to Danny as he patted her back.

"It's okay, lady," Danny said as he held on to her. "Do you want some gum?"

At these words, Goldilocks moaned in despair and pulled herself from Danny's embrace, her face wet with her own tears.

She continued to sob, and for the first time since becoming this person she had created for herself, this shell inside which she hid from the world, this ... *Goldilocks*, she began to see the mistake she had made of her life. She looked to the three bears before her and felt shame, and it burned so hot that she flinched.

"Are you alright, dear?" The female bear asked.

Goldilocks wasn't sure how to answer. She was suddenly confused. Why was she here? Lucy would never do anything like this.

No, but Goldilocks would.

But who was she?

Was she Goldilocks or Lucy?

She didn't know anymore. In her confusion she took a step backwards up the staircase and away from the bears.

"Goldilocks?" The female bear said, taking a step toward her.

"No! Not Goldilocks! Never again!" and with that, Lucy Goodnight turned, ran up the staircase, and disappeared deeper into Griswold House.

CHAPTER NINETEEN

THE BEAST WOKE ALONE in the room with three chairs. He sat up and took a moment to get his bearings. His head hurt and what looked like a wooden rocking chair lay in pieces all around him.

She hit me with a chair, he thought to himself, rubbing the back of his head, which was still rather tender.

He stood and his legs began to wobble. Everything around him was blurred and distorted, as if he viewed the world through lenses made from the bottoms of glass soda bottles. So he sat back down. And then, because it seemed like the right thing to do, he passed out ... again.

While unconscious he spent some more time with the colorful singing badgers who made him promises of chocolates, comfy sheets, large quantities of mayonnaise, and a long life of happiness, joy, and unending pain. This last one he felt to be most unsettling.

The Beast regained consciousness once again and thought it might be best this time to take things a little slow. He crawled over to the large recliner and pulled himself into it, marveling at the way it truly conformed to his body and cradled his spine. He'd have to get one for his place once this was all over.

He sat in silence for a time. Listening to the sounds of the house around him. Trying to clear his mind and settle on his next course of action.

His dream with the field of yellow roses had been both revealing and somewhat disturbing. Did the yellow field represent Goldilocks? Did the bear represent the family that owned this house? They were bears, after all. But he wasn't sure. He didn't buy in to all that dream interpretation claptrap. There is an entire field of study out there that believes dreams can teach you things about yourself that you've never known before. That dreams are the way your subconscious self-communicates to you and tells you what it is you truly want out of life, and people use this information to make life changing decisions.

The Beast didn't buy it. As far as he was concerned, dreams were just a way for your subconscious self to get rid of all the visual and oral stimuli you were subjected to each day from television, radio, the internet; pretty much everywhere. Dreams were nothing more than your brain taking an informational dump each night and ejecting all the worthless crap it had been filled with each day.

Yet, he did have to admit to himself that he may still have feelings for Goldilocks. Despite her betrayal and the anger he felt, he still cared for her. Granted, he just tried to kill her, but these things happen in even the healthiest of relationships.

The Beast pulled his gun, a Smith & Wesson Model M&P R8. It was black with a synthetic grip. It held eight .357 Magnum rounds and had a five inch barrel. He loved the gun. Well, love might be too strong of a word, but he sure felt good holding it in his hand. He swung out the cylinder and pulled out each cartridge, then reloaded. The act gave him comfort.

Just then he heard a scream from somewhere in the house. A woman's scream. Goldilocks.

The Beast leaped to his feet, fighting off a wave of dizziness and nausea, not giving even a second thought to the idea that he might have a concussion. He holstered his pistol and ran from the room, making for the direction in which the scream had come.

It took him a few moments to find Goldilocks. The house was huge, but he found her all the same. She was at the top of a staircase at the front of the house. He noticed three potential problems the instant Goldilocks came into view.

Potential Problem Number One: A rather large bear stood between Goldilocks and himself.

Potential Problem Number Two: Another rather large bear was with the first rather large bear, and they both stood between Goldilocks and himself.

Potential Problem Number Three: A smaller bear, but large all the same, stood just behind the two rather large bears that stood between Goldilocks and himself.

Luckily the three bears hadn't yet noticed him. Goldilocks hadn't noticed him yet either. She just sat there on the floor above him. She looked miserable. She looked sad. She looked reflective and regretful.

She looked beautiful.

The smaller of the three bears suddenly advanced on Goldilocks. The Beast drew his gun, but the bear, instead of mauling her, gave her a hug. The Beast was confused. Then Goldilocks began to cry, and with that he had had enough. He was not about to sit idly by while Goldilocks received the comfort and care that he deserved. *He* was the one who was betrayed. *He* was the one who suffered. *He* was the one who had died a little inside. At the same time, he didn't like that bear touching her, even if it was innocent. He suddenly felt protective. He wanted to be the one to comfort her. To protect her. To touch her, hold her, be with her. He needed her.

He still loved her. And frankly, that just plain pissed him off.

With his gun in one hand, he drew his sword and just as he was about to call out something powerful and dramatic like "Get away from her," Goldilocks began to shout.

"No! Not Goldilocks! Never again!" and with that, she turned, ran up the staircase, and disappeared deeper into the house.

"Well crap," the big bear said. "I guess that means we gotta chase her."

The three bears set off up the staircase after Goldilocks, none of them noticing that a man with a pistol and a sword stood behind them. The Beast stepped forward to take chase when his head began to spin and the world around him went all squishy.

A scarlet badger came bounding down the steps and stopped at the feet of the Beast, looking up at him with an expression that on a human could only be described as shifty, but on a badger ... well, still looked rather shifty.

"Hey, fella," the badger said. "You need any socks?"

"What?"

"Socks, guy? You need any socks?"

He noticed that the badger wore a long overcoat. The badger opened it up and revealed row upon row of pristine white socks hanging on the inner lining.

The Beast wobbled slightly and vertigo took hold of him and he fell onto his back. As he slid back into unconsciousness, as he mentally calculated the possibility of purchasing a comfortable pair of woolly socks, he heard Goldilocks crying out in absolute terror from somewhere above. So he fought. He clawed and he spit. He cursed and he bit. He fought free from whatever tried to pull him into oblivion. He fought, and he won. The scarlet badger was no more.

The Beast sat up and shook the cobwebs from his head. His gun lay to one side, his sword to the other. He picked up his gun and sword and stood. He wasn't sure where in the house Goldilocks and the three bears had gone, but he could hear people running above, moving deeper into the interior of the house, so he launched himself up the steps. He paused at the top, listening. All he heard was nothing.

Then the nothing was replaced with something.

The something was the sound of gunfire from outside on the front lawn. Gunfire and people screaming. The sound lasted for almost two minutes before it resolved into the thud of boot heels falling on concrete as someone walked up the sidewalk outside toward the front door. The sound was accompanied by a feeling of great evil. A feeling so intense that he wanted to vomit. Such evil that the Beast, who had known fear before, discovered what true terror felt like.

So he turned and ran. Hoping against hope that he would find Goldilocks. Find her and tell her that he still loved her. Tell her before they all died.

CHAPTER TWENTY

ALBERT GORDON, GRIMMELTON FIREFIGHTER and all around smarmy guy, was not in a good mood. Al had one motivation in life, an extreme dedication to meeting girls. He devoted great swaths of time, money, and energy to the task. Entire days were planned months in advance toward this one venture. Al had even signed up to be a volunteer firefighter for the sole purpose of getting girls to take an interest in him. The only problem with the whole firefighting gig was that Al had a paralyzing fear of fire. Luckily, one of the more interesting facts about Grimmelton, Kansas was that there hadn't been a fire in town since 1983. "Fire free since '83," most Gimmeltonions were known to say when they set about to brag on their home town. So Al felt pretty safe making the leap into firefighting when there were no actual fires to fight.

See, Al knew, or at least he had a fairly good idea, that the ladies just love a man in uniform, so while Al didn't have to actually go out and fight any fires, he often got the opportunity to respond to a plethora of emergency situations. When eight year old Timmy Brosco fell into that well last month, Al was there with the team that pulled the boy out. When the Cleaver boy climbed into that giant coffee cup on the billboard above the downtown market six months ago, Al was on the scene. When that same idiot Cleaver kid got his head stuck between the bars of a wrought iron fence two days later, Al was there to grease the kid's ears. So no, Al didn't have to put out any fires, but he did get to suit up and look like a hero as often as possible, and of course, get the ladies.

There weren't many occasions in which the firefighter gig worked against Al. Usually it only came back to bite him on his butt when he had to be pulled away from working his magic on a babe just so he could stand around in his firefighter's gear and do nothing. Most especially when there weren't any girls around to impress.

Today happened to be one of those occasions.

Al had been out at the Chicken Coup on Route 9, playing pool, drinking beer, and of course, doing what he did best ... hitting on chicks. There weren't too many women at the bar this time of the day, being early afternoon and all, but that meant that there weren't too many fellas around to compete with either.

But it wasn't just any random girl Al had been trying to score with this morning. Al spent most of his afternoons at the Chicken Coup lately for one reason only. The new waitress. Rose.

Al didn't know much about Rose. Only that she used to be married to someone powerful and important. He knew that she left him, but wasn't sure why. He honestly didn't care. He also knew that Rose wasn't her first name. It was her last name, and her maiden one at that. He had no idea what her first name was. She only went by Rose. He didn't know much about the woman, but that was okay by him. He felt that he already knew all he really needed to know about Rose. He knew that she was the most beautiful woman he had ever seen. He knew that she seemed to enjoy the attention that he gave her. And he knew that he couldn't stop thinking about her. That was really all he needed.

Al had been on the verge of convincing Rose that going out to dinner with him sometime would be one of the all-time great ideas in the history of great ideas when his phone rang. He looked down at the display window and saw that it was Chief Rudolph, which meant that he was being called into duty. He apologized, kissed Rose's hand, and left with a heavy heart.

Which was how he found himself sitting on his rear, in the grass, in full gear, in the heat, out in front of Griswold House, doing nothing at all, and with no girls around to impress.

Al Gordon was not in a good mood.

Twenty minutes ago the fire alarm at Griswold House had sounded. All able bodied volunteer firefighters were dispatched with a speed that would have made the Flash look like an old man standing on his lawn screaming at passing cars to slow the heck down. But by the time they had arrived, the fire alarm had quieted. There were no signs of fire, and no one had answered neither the phone, nor the front door, which was locked. The staff were all out on the front lawn, but the Griswold family were nowhere to be found. So, Chief Rudolph, ever the one to avoid displeasing the wealthy, chose to just sit and wait. The household staff were no help. No one among them would take any initiative. They deferred to the family, or when they weren't around, to the head of security, Jack Horner. And of course, Jack was annoyingly absent as well.

When the Griswold family finally showed, Al was relieved. At last he'd be able to leave. Maybe Rose was still at the Chicken Coup.

But it was not to be.

As soon as the Griswold family arrived, the security guy, Jack came out of the house. To Al, the man looked injured. He went straight for the Griswolds. The big bear, Al thought his name was Burt, or Bud ... maybe Burt, called for a medic and the EMTs that were on the scene grabbed their bags and went to work. All the while Mr. Griswold and the security guy talked. Jack must have said something to Burt, Bud, or whatever his name was, to get him riled up because suddenly the bear stood, said something to his wife, and all three of the bears started for the house.

Al noticed Chief Rudolph running to intercept the Griswolds, and Al decided to join them.

"Excuse me," the Chief called as he ran. "Excuse me, Burt?" That was the bear's name. Burt.

The big bear, Burt, turned and stopped. His wife and kid waited with him as the Chief and Al caught up.

The Chief asked, "What would you like us to do, Burt?"

"Do about what?" Burt looked distracted, like he had somewhere else he'd rather be.

"About the fire alarm," Al said. "The alarm went off. We got a fire to fight here or what?" Al prayed silently that they did not, in fact, have a fire to fight here.

"It was a false alarm," Burt said. "There is no fire."

"Good, so we can go." Al thought the day might be looking up.

"No," Burt said. "I'd like you to stay."

"But, Burt, without a fire, what do you want us to do?" The Chief asked.

"There may be a thief on the premises. There's no telling what she might do. I'd appreciate it if you all just stood ready. Just in case." And with that, the Griswold's entered the house.

"Can you believe that?" Al said. "Who does that guy think he is? We ain't his own private team of first responders. We got better things to do than just sit and wait. I mean, come on!"

"Now, Al," the Chief said. "Burt's a good man – I mean, bear. He's done a lot for this community."

"And he's given a lot of money to the fire department," Al finished the thought for him.

"Well, yes, that's true. But we're going to stay. If Burt and his family need our help, then I'm going make sure that we're here for them." The Chief walked away to inform the rest of the crew, which left Al with nothing to do but wait.

Al took a moment to scan the household staff. They had all broken off into little groups that were spread out all over the front lawn. He was, as some call it, 'scoping for chicks'. Al figured, if he was going to be stuck here in the heat with his uniform and gear on, he might as well take advantage of it. Al found just what he was looking for a few moments later. The housemaids.

Al approached the small knot of housemaids who were all standing about and talking in excited voices on the same subject everyone else seemed to be talking about. The non-fire and the possible thief in the Griswold's home.

"Who is she?" one of the more attractive housemaids asked to the group.

"Does it matter," another replied. "Someone needs to go in there and get her."

"But, what if she's dangerous. I heard she beat up Jack!" the first one squealed in fright.

"Never fear, ladies. The Grimmelton Fire Department is on the scene," Al said, striking his best Superman pose.

Al noticed one of the housemaids roll her eyes ... he didn't find her all that attractive. He was about to respond to the eye roll when something exploded from down the road. The ground shook slightly beneath them and a bulbous cloud of oily smoke rose up on the horizon. It looked to Al like it might be coming from the Brick House Gas and Groceries. Maybe one of their wells blew. Al couldn't be sure.

Regardless, every firefighter, police officer, and EMT on site froze for a moment or two before springing into action.

"Ladies," Al said, tipping his helmet in salute and giving the housemaids his very best smile before jogging off to join his crew.

But before Al could climb aboard his assigned fire truck, he noticed a figure walking up the road, walking out of the wall of smoke that billowed toward Al and the others. The figure was dressed in black. Black boots, hat, pants, coat, and string tie over a shirt of white. The man looked like he stepped out of an old western. Gunsmoke, Rawhide, or even Bonanza. He looked like the sort of character that frequented a saloon and always had a fan of cards in one hand and a shot glass in the other. He even wore a pair of old revolvers.

No one moved as the man drew closer. Al and the rest just sat in, or hung on, to their vehicles, letting the engines run.

As the man in black drew nearer, one of the police officers climbed out of his cruiser and stepped over to the man, barring his way. They were too far from Al, so he couldn't hear what they were saying, but the conversation didn't last long. The officer made a gesture to get the man to stop. The man pulled one of his revolvers, and without slowing, shot the officer down, stepped over the body, and continued moving toward the house.

Al couldn't believe what he'd just seen. His mouth had gone dry and his bladder threatened to let go. Al was no stranger to violence, but he was only use to the kind created by Hollywood. Al had never before born witness to the callus, almost casual way in which the man in black took the life of another. It was like a child stepping on a beetle. The act clearly meant nothing to this dark stranger.

The man in black drew closer. All that stood between him and the house were pretty much every emergency vehicle and worker in town, minus the few police officers that responded to a call for back up down at the Brick House – which was where this man had come from. Al looked at the smoke on the horizon, the smoke that appeared to hang directly over the location of the Brick House. What had happened down there?

The man in black drew near. He smiled and said, "Ladies and gentlemen, allow me to introduce myself. I am death, and death am I."

Al felt cold. The man in black didn't raise his voice, he didn't shout, and he certainly wasn't close enough for Al to hear him without doing one or the other, but Al heard him all the same.

"Now, I don't want to take up any more of your time," the man in black continued, "but I have business there in yonder house, and I'd truly appreciate it if y'all just stepped aside so that I may continue forth."

Al looked to the people around him and found that they were all doing the same as him.

"I will not ask again," the man in black said, his eyes going dark like coal. "There are limits to my good nature. You will move, or I will gun you all down were you stand and simply step over your lifeless bodies as I have done with your constable back there."

No one moved.

The man in black pulled both revolvers, thumbed back the hammers, and said, "I did warn you."

"Put them down, mister!" It was Jack Horner. He had stepped out from the back of an ambulance, a bandage wrapped around his head. He had his own gun drawn. It was one of those dark and blocky hand guns that all the best special agents and cops used in all the best television shows.

Al gaped as the man in black laughed, dropping his arms to his side and affecting a relaxed and carefree posture.

"Walk on, son," the man said, a smile on his face. "I'm fresh out of warnings."

Jack didn't hesitate and opened fire. Three quick shots that took the man in black once in the head and twice in the chest. The man fell. Al jumped back in surprise.

That's it? Al thought as the sound of the three shots echoed off into the distance to be replaced by the shocked silence of those around him. He wasn't prepared for the suddenness of it all. He would only have to wait a few more seconds however, to see that *that*, was most definitely not *it*.

"It's over, folks," Jack said, turning to Al and the crowd around him. "Now," he paused, sliding the gun back into its holder under his shoulder. "I need five officers to accompany me into Griswold House."

Men in uniform began to step forward as something stirred behind Jack. It was the man in black, who was still very much alive.

The man in black rose in a way that would never be mistaken for dramatic. He just simply pulled himself to his feet, groaning as old men do when they pull themselves out of a recliner. He brushed himself off, his revolvers still in his hands, tsking away like being shot three times was just one of those annoying things that one had to put up with on a daily basis, like being stuck in traffic, or seeing your computer freezing up.

Jack spun, drawing his gun as he turned. His movements were fluid, it was like ballet with Jack. Al began to gain a respect for Jack Horner that just wasn't there before. Sure, he didn't really know the man, but Al could see that Jack was the sort of guy that he would want at his back when the crap began to fall. Like, well. Like today.

"Stand down!" Jack fell naturally into a shooter's stance, his gun in both hands. If he was at all fazed by the man in black's miraculous resurrection he sure didn't let it show. Al found respect in that as well.

The man in black didn't respond with words. His retort was quick, sudden, and final. One shot and Jack dropped, never to move again.

"I am through playing around," the man in black said, turning to the officers who had stepped forward at Jack's request.

The man in black opened fire. Al had never seen anything like it. The man shot, over and over, never reloading, a never ending stream of bullets flying steadily forth as the people around him scattered. No one made it far before they were shot down. Every shot hit its mark, some finding more than one as the bullets sought out their targets, going through one body and then another. Some shots even appeared to curve, turning in midair as they exited one victim to take down whomever had been running alongside them.

The air grew thick with the sound of gunfire, the whine of the bullets, and the screams of the dying. Al had dropped to the ground and covered his head in his hands as everyone around him died. He knew it would just be a matter of time before he would be next.

Then, as suddenly as it had begun, it was over. To Al it was a lifetime, but in reality, the carnage lasted no more than two minutes. One hundred and twenty seconds, and fifty three people lay dead. Wives, husbands, fathers, sons, mothers, and daughters; people who were loved, who were needed, and who would be missed. All gone. All silenced forever with the squeezing of a trigger.

In the end Al found himself alone with the man in black. Al hadn't moved. Fear had kept him rooted to the spot. Al looked to the man in black, the man who had called himself death, and the man in black smiled, showing teeth that were as dark as his eyes had become.

The man in black pointed both pistols at Al, and Al heard the man speak one last time. "I did warn them," the man said, and then he squeezed the triggers.

Al's last thought as he was cast into oblivion was of Rose, the waitress at the Chicken Coup out on Route 9. He wished he'd had a chance to find out what it would have felt like to kiss that woman, just once, and then he was no more.

♦　♦　♦　♦　♦

What once was an unorganized mash up of parked fire trucks, police cruisers, ambulances, first responders, and household staff, was now nothing more than a feast for the crows, maggots, and other creatures that found life from the deaths of others.

Only the man in black, who called himself Doc, was left standing.

Doc blew smoke out of the barrels of each pistol, holstered both, and started toward the house, walking casually with a feline grace as he stepped over that which he had wrought.

"I did warn them," Doc said aloud before he began to whistle a jaunty tune that sounded a bit like the theme song to *I Love Lucy*.

A moment later Doc was at the front door to Griswold House. He paused a moment and pulled a thin cigar from inside his coat. He produced a small box of wooden matches from the same pocket, struck one of the matches on the side of the box, and used it to light the cigar with great puffs.

After taking a few moments to enjoy his cigar, Doc reared back and kicked the door with such force that it didn't just burst off the hinges, two feet of the wall surrounding the door went with it. The door and wall flew into the house, the door breaking into pieces on the main staircase.

Doc crossed the threshold and stood in the foyer of Griswold House, looking about with a smile on his face. He cupped a hand to the side of his mouth and called out in a voice that could be heard in every corner of the sprawling mansion, "Oh Lucy, I'm home!"

CHAPTER
TWENTY-ONE

L UCY GOODNIGHT LED THE three bears on a merry chase through the upper levels of the house. She ran and the bears followed.

She hadn't gone far when the sound of splintering wood was heard from the front of the house, causing Lucy to stop and listen.

The three bears had just caught up to her, huffing and puffing from the run, when a voice sounded all around them. A voice that Lucy found all too familiar. A voice that filled her veins with ice.

"Oh Lucy, I'm home!" the voice cried out and surrounded them as if the very air had become sound.

"No!" Lucy cried out.

"Who was that, Mommy?" the small bear rubbed at his ears with his fists.

"Goldilocks?" the big male bear asked, reaching out to take her arm.

But Goldilocks, Lucy, pulled free as the panic set it.

"Oh, God no!" Lucy yelled. "He's here! He's found me! Oh, God! Please, no!" And with that, she turned and ran even deeper into the house.

She had no idea where she was going, she just ran. She had no plan. No scheme. No clever trick or ruse that could get her clear from this place, or from this moment. She just ran.

Her only thought, her only motivation, her sole purpose in life at this moment in time was to get as far away as possible. Far away from him. So she ran.

She couldn't think. She couldn't reason. She only knew panic. Panic and disbelief. She thought she had made a clean escape. She thought that she was free. She wasn't. He had found her. Her husband, Doc, had found her. And for the first time in years, she truly remembered what fear felt like. So she ran.

She could hear the bears following her as she made her way deeper into the house, choosing paths at random. The bears were yelling her name, shouting for her to stop, but she wouldn't listen. She wasn't about to stop. They didn't understand. No one understood what she had gone through all those years with him. What he had done. What she had been made to suffer. Nobody understood but her. Well, her and Doc. And the Devil too, she supposed.

So she ran. Her fear building with each step.

Fear is a great motivator and teaching tool, second only to pain. You get fear and pain together, take them out for a few drinks, let them spend some good quality time really getting to know each other, and with a team like that at your side, there isn't much you can't accomplish.

The team of Fear and Pain is not infallible, however. Lucy is proof of that. She had spent years under their collective thumb, guided by her husband. She had suffered under his torture, both physical and emotional. Living with the fear that made up the bars of her cage. Living with the pain that was the lock.

Yet, in the end, Lucy had found the will to resist. In the end, she had found something deep within her that had very well had enough, and so she had left. Everyone had a line. A line that they have placed between what they will and what they will not accept. Doc had crossed that line.

But the fear was still there. And so Lucy ran like a woman possessed. She made two right turns, three left turns, another right, and then two more lefts. She found a flight of stairs and went up them, turning left at the top. She ran through rooms with televisions, couches, and lamps. She ran through rooms with exercise equipment. She ran through bathrooms, a large room containing an Olympic sized swimming pool, and a library with more books on the shelves than Lucy had ever seen.

Lucy suddenly found herself at the end of a long hallway. Before her rose a door stretching to the ceiling. A door so large that one might find its twin on the house at the top of Jack's beanstalk. The sheer size of the door intrigued Lucy, and for a time, her fear vanished. And then, for just a moment, Lucy wondered, in a whimsical sort of way, if a giant gorilla might live in the room beyond the great door. She smiled as the thought occurred to her.

Regardless, just looking at the thing, Lucy realized she wasn't going through the door. Not without a little finesse, a bit of luck, and a thermonuclear bomb. The door gave off an air of impenetrability that even Gandalf the Grey would respect and no Balrog would dare debate. It didn't have a handle, only a 10-digit electronic keypad. The door left Lucy with a choice to make. Go back the way she had come, or fall to the floor in defeat and just give the whole thing up.

While a part of her felt some comfort in the whole "giving up" idea, Lucy decided to soldier on. Because, while fear and pain, the two great motivators, had kept her in her husband's clutches for all those years, the two worked just as hard now to keep her out. But before Lucy could move, the three bears came jogging around the corner at the other end of the hall, trapping her with her back to the door to King Kong's room.

"Goldilocks," the female bear said. "Thank God."

"Where are you running to, girl?" asked the big male.

"You need to move," Lucy said, trying to push past the bears.

"Now hold on there, missy," the big male said, grabbing her by her left wrist.

Lucy swung around and punched the big bear right on the nose. He yelled in pain, but didn't let go of her arm.

"Dangit, girl!" the big male shouted.

Lucy punched him again.

"Stop it!," he yelled.

Lucy punched him again. Or at least she tried. This time the big male was ready. He caught her other wrist. Then he lifted her into the air. He held her there, her feet dangling off the floor, and brought her to eye level.

"Now," the bear said, "before you get to thinking about kicking me somewhere that might seriously disappoint my wife, know that I will pull both of your arms from their sockets if you try."

Lucy believed him. She could see by the look in his eyes that he could, and would, do exactly as he threatened.

"You ready to stop running and let us try and help you?" the bear asked, still holding her off of the ground. "If you are, I'll let you down."

Lucy nodded, a frown on her face.

"Okay then," the bear said, setting her down. "Why don't we try this all over again. My name is Burt." He held his hand out to her.

Lucy took the bear's hand, Burt's hand. She could have fit two of her hands in his. They shook and she said, "I'm Goldilocks, well ... Lucy. Goldilocks is a lie."

"I don't understand," Burt said, his brow furrowing in thought.

"It's really too long of a story to explain, and we don't have time now that he's found me. Please we need to leave," the panic had begun to set in again.

"Goldilocks, or Lucy, or whatever, I believe in doing things right and proper. There is time for introductions and explanations," he then gestured to the female bear behind him. "This here pretty lady behind me is my wife, Beatrice."

Beatrice and Lucy shook hands as Lucy looked about her, wondering when Doc would turn the corner beyond the bears.

"And this handsome young man," said Burt, gesturing for the smaller bear to come forward. "Is our boy, Danny."

Lucy held her hand out to shake, but Danny pushed past her hand and enveloped her in a hug, just like before. The hug made

Lucy feel ... well, great, and for a moment, her fear vanished and she felt safe. There was something so purely genuine about the hug that she just couldn't resist hugging back.

Then Danny let go, and went to hide behind his mother again.

"Alright then, now that we know each other, why don't you tell us what this is all about," Burt said. "What are you running from?"

"It's complicated."

"Try me."

"Does it have anything to do with that handsome young man with the sword we saw in the Brick House parking lot," said Beatrice.

"Him? No, that's Tim. He's, well . . . he *was* my boyfriend," Lucy said.

"Is that who you are running from?" Burt asked.

"No, not really. I mean, yes, he's chasing me. But he's not who I'm running from. He's only chasing me *because* I'm running." Lucy said with a smile that showed she knew it sounded silly.

"Okay," said Burt. "So who are you running from?"

"Doc Holliday."

Burt laughed.

"It's not a joke," Lucy said.

"Wait a minute," Burt said. "Doc Holliday? *The* Doc Holliday? Like, the guy with the Earps and the O.K. Corral? The guy that died over a hundred years ago? *That* Doc Holliday?"

"Yes," said Goldilocks, looking down. "He's my husband."

"Your husband!?" A voice shouted behind her.

Lucy turned. Standing there at the other end of the hall, a look of shock and betrayal on his face, was Tim, the Beast.

"Tim," said Lucy, stepping toward him, guilt in her voice.

"No," the Beast said, holding one hand out before him, the other covering his face. "No, don't." He staggered, took a couple of steps back, and for the third time that day, passed out, crumpling into a heap on the floor.

CHAPTER TWENTY-TWO

JOHN HENRY 'DOC' HOLLIDAY died of tuberculosis at the age of thirty-six in Glenwood Springs, Colorado, on November 8th, 1887.

It was then that his new life had begun.

It has been said that on the day that Doc Holliday died, God and the Devil fought for possession of his soul.

The Devil won.

Doc was a man who, when alive, walked a line each and every day. A thin line between good and evil. Doc had within him the potential to do much good, but also the potential to do great evil. Doc was noble, yet cruel. Loyal to his friends, yet unmerciful to his enemies. Doc Holliday had a dark side, which was apparent to anyone who knew him. And the Devil wanted that dark side. The Devil had plans for John Henry "Doc" Holliday.

And so, on the day that he had passed from this world, Doc Holliday was taken into the fiery pits of Hell. There he spent the next fifty years in agony as Hell's minions reshaped him. Blackened his soul. Changed him by removing from him that which was unwanted and enhancing that which Hell found desirable.

The denizens of Hell began their work on Doc by erasing his compassion, his nobility, everything in him that had the potential to make him a good man, exorcising it completely from his being. Then they upgraded those qualities within him that could, and would, be used for evil. His willingness to kill. His bloodlust. His cruelty and selfishness. All the traits that made the name 'Doc Holliday' strike fear in men and woman all throughout the Old West.

When Hell was done with him, Doc Holliday no longer resembled the man who stood by the side of Wyatt Earp, putting his life on the line to help his friend. That Doc would recognize certain aspects of the new Doc's nature, but the old version would be afraid of the new. Doc was no longer a man. Doc was a creature of Hell.

His new role, his new reason for being, was to create chaos on Earth. To seek out evil and nurture it, raise it up to destroy and kill and all the nasty stuff that evil likes to do.

And he was good at it.

Doc Holliday had his hand in almost every criminal enterprise in the world. He was Doctor Doom, Lex Luther, Keyser Soze, and Darth Vader all rolled into one body. He was smart, cultured, cunning, good looking, imaginative, and most importantly, quite evil. And his power was immense. Doc could now tap into abilities the average person only knew from reading Sci-Fi novels.

Doc Holliday was a ghost, a phantom, a mystery, and a legend. He was the monster under your bed. The boogie man in your closet. The FBI had a file on him so big that it had its own floor in their headquarters at Quantico. Yet they had no idea who he was. The CIA knew of him only by reputation, and had been known to send work his way from time to time.

More than one world leader owes their position to Doc. Prime Ministers, Presidents, Queens, Doc has ways to get to each and every one of them if necessary. Doc has his finger over the button. He has the whole world in the palm of his hand – and all he has to do is squeeze to end all life on the face of the planet. But that's not why he is among us. After all, Evil cannot thrive without life.

One rainy day in June, Doc met a young lady named Lucy. The circumstances of their meeting are not important. Suffice it to say, that when Doc first laid eyes upon her, he discovered himself to be quite taken.

Lucy was petite, somewhat bookish, and rather plain. But Doc saw the beauty within her. He could see the radiance that shown from her, a light that most overlooked, or simply could not see. Doc discovered feelings within him that he'd not know in a great while.

She would be his prize. He would take her and show her off like a bauble from his shelf. He would take her down when he needed her, and put her back when he didn't. She would be his. Completely.

So Doc wooed her. He really turned on the charm. Doc could be rather smooth when he wanted to be. It's easy to get someone to fall in love with you when you had the power to lie with such sincerity.

Doc's plan was simple. If you want a girl to fall for you, it must be for you. Not your money. Not your power. She had to fall for who you are. Or in Doc's case, who you pretended to be. He played the role of a starving artist, a musician with a heart of gold and the soul of a poet. And she fell for it. She fell hard.

Soon the two were wed and Doc revealed his true self to his new bride. She was, understandably, quiet taken aback. But it was too late. He had her. Mind, body, and soul.

Or so he thought.

Six years into their marriage, she disappeared. Doc was furious. No one walked away from him. No one. He had to find her. She had to be made to see her error in judgment. Then she had to die, and she had to die horribly. She had to be made an example of so that others would know the price of betrayal. Of betraying him. But what angered him most, what he found to be quite disturbing was the realization that he did, in fact, have feelings for the girl. That wasn't supposed to happen. And Doc had to do something about it.

It took nearly three years and every resource at his command, but in the end she was spotted by a rat in his employ by the name of Phil. She was on the other side of the country. She'd changed her name, her hair, her entire person to escape him. And it had almost worked.

The moment he had learned that she had been found, Doc realized that he had to handle this one personally. He also understood that he had to go old school on this one. And so he dressed in the manner of his old self. Boots, hat, guns, and all. He was the Doc Holliday out of legend. He was death.

He would find his Lucy. He would find her, and when he did, she would die. And so would any who got in his way.

CHAPTER
TWENTY-THREE

ER HUSBAND!? THE BEAST thought just a fraction of a second before he yelled, "Your husband!?"

A few seconds later he was unconscious on the floor. Again.

The amount of thought that can go through your head in just a few seconds is actually quite staggering. This is what went through the Beast's head between the moment he yelled, "Your husband!?" and the moment he fell into his deep sleep:

She's married?

Married!?

Like, married-married?

Married!?

Seriously? This isn't something she could have told me during the two years we were together?

I mean, we got married ... right?

Hold the phone! Does this mean that we aren't married because she was already married!?

What do they call that, anyway? Polymorph? Polygram? Polygamy? That's it, polygamy.

Am I a polygamist!?

No, I can't be. Goldilocks is though, considering that she was married already.

Married.

Married!?

MARRIED!

You know what? Married is one of those words that really start to sound silly when you say it too much.

Married, married, married, married, married, married. It's lost all meaning to me now.

Look at her over there. She's so pretty. Goldilocks and Tim. Tim and Goldilocks. Forever and ever.

I'd like to go back to calling myself Tim someday.

I wonder what her husband is like. I bet he's a real jerk.

I bet I could take him.

I'd kick his butt then blow him up.

It's been a while since I've blown anything up. I'd like to blow something up today.

I like explosions.

What's up with those bears?

Are they protecting her? Should I protect her from them?

I fought a bear in my dream. I understand that if you curl up in the fetal position during a bear attack that they'll leave you alone. I wonder if that bear guy did that when he was attacked.

You know the bear guy right? The bear guy? He's the guy who went to live will all the bears. Then they ate him. That must have sucked.

I hope I never get eaten. What a crappy way to go.

I'm hungry.

I haven't eaten all day.

Is that lobster bisque I smell?

Ugh! I can't stand sea food.

I could really go for a burrito right now.

Or a taco.

I've always wanted to try a chalupa.

She really is pretty. Her hair, her eyes. Oh, but it's her smile. Her smile makes my heart beat, like really fast.

What's up with that door? It's freaking huge! What, are they keeping King Kong back there?

You know, I'm really happy with Peter Jackson's remake of King Kong. The dinosaurs looked fake, but dang did that gorilla look real. And I felt for the thing. I knew how it was going to end, yet still hoped for the best. THAT'S how you make a movie.

She looks scared. Why would Goldilocks be scared? Oh yeah, her husband. He must be one scary dude to get her all worked up. I've never known her to be scared of anything.

Of course, I guess I don't know her that well anymore, do I?

I thought she loved me, but she lied. The entire time we were together she was lying.

I still love her. I can't help it. Look at her. My heart aches to hold her again.

"Tim," said Goldilocks, stepping toward him, guilt in her voice.

Oh yeah, right. Now she's going to act all concerned and guilty. I'll show her!

"No," the Beast said, holding one hand out before him, the other covering his face. "No, don't."

Yeah, take that! Woo!

I wonder if they have a Taco Bell in this town. I could really go for a taco. Meat, cheese, sour cream. No veggies. That's what I'm talking about.

Maybe Goldilocks would want a taco ... or maybe even a chalupa.

No, wait. She's married.

MARRIED!

What. A Pisser.

I need a beer.

Wait a minute! Am I fainting?

Again!?

Come on! What's going on with this day!?

Can't a guy catch a break!?

I still love her. She makes me a better person.

I love you Goldilocks!

The Beast staggered, took a couple of steps back, and for the third time that day, passed out, crumpling into a heap on the floor.

CHAPTER TWENTY-FOUR

OFFICER CARL FRIENDLY ARRIVED at Griswold House in time to see the man in black kick in the Griswold's front door.

Carl was stunned, to say the least. He was stupefied, baffled, befuddled, bemused, bewildered, mystified, perplexed, puzzled, taken aback, and any other words that meant the same as 'confused'.

All around him lay the bodies of friends, colleagues, and strangers. More than he was willing to count. He'd never seen the kind of violence he'd been made to behold today, and it had just started to catch up to him. He didn't know how to take it all in, how to process what he'd seen.

His coworkers, some of which he'd considered friends, were dead and had been left to rot in the sun where they lay. So Carl did what most men would do. Carl wept.

And then he prayed.

He dropped to his knees, buried his face in his hands and cried. His tears flowed like the waters of the mighty Mississippi. He cried soft and muffled cries. He cried loud and braying cries. His cries were those of a man whose faith had been all but shattered.

But then he prayed.

Carl considered himself a good man. He believed in God. He hadn't stepped through the doors of a church since he was a kid, but he still believed.

And so, for the first time in years, Carl prayed. Right there on the front lawn of Griswold House, with death all around him. Carl asked God why. Why did this have to happen? Why did these people have to die? Why would God allow such a person like Doc to walk the Earth? Carl asked for a little understanding.

Then Carl was blinded by a light that surrounded and enveloped him.

And out of this light walked a small figure. He couldn't make the person out, just a vaguely humanoid blob. The light seemed to be radiating from this figure.

Then, as suddenly as it had appeared, the light went out, and before Carl stood a little girl. She looked to be about five, possibly six. Her hair was the color of old wood left in the sun, and it was tied up in no less than seven short pony-tails that stuck up all over her head. The rest of her hair reached just short of her chin, while her bangs brushed the tops of her eyebrows. She wore a pink t-shirt with a white star centered across the chest, blue jeans, and white sneakers. She looked at Carl and smiled.

"Hi, Carl," she said. "You and I need to have us a little talk."

Carl stood, his legs threatening to fail. He wiped the tears from his eyes with the backs of his hands and said, "Who're you?"

"I am who I am," She replied, smiling.

"W-what?"

"Look, Carl. We don't really have time for all of this. You know who I am. I know who I am. Okay? So let's get down to the nitty-gritty here. Alright?"

"Okay."

"Good, now why don't you sit down before you fall down. What do you say there, huh sport?"

"Okay." Carl feared that he might be going insane. He was in a daze as he tried to make sense of his day. So far it proved difficult. In the end he found it easier to just give in. So he sat. The girl stood in front of him. The two were at eye level.

"Okay then," she said. "Here's the deal. There is a very bad man here, Carl. A very bad man. You understand that, right?"

"Bad man."

"There you go," she said, smiling as she put a comforting hand on his shoulder. "Now, this bad man, he calls himself Doc. You with me so far there, Carl?"

"Bad man. Doc."

"You got it. Doc is a very bad man. A bad man who was put here by an old employee of mine. The two of us don't see eye-to-eye on much anymore, and I'm afraid he does what he can to try and ruin those things that I have worked a lifetime to create. You following me?"

"I think so."

"I need your help, Carl."

"Me?"

"You bet."

Carl looked at the bodies around him on the lawn. This just couldn't be happening. He rubbed his eyes with his fists and sighed loudly. He looked back at the girl.

"Who are you?" he asked again.

She slapped him. Hard. Right across the face.

Carl once watched a video online. A video where a group of people recorded a man getting slapped across the face in a very controlled, scientific-like environment. Then they played it back at super slow motion. The man's face seemed to bend in upon itself in a way that faces just shouldn't do. His nose – Carl will never forget the man's nose – looked like it folded back onto his face at such an extreme angle that there just wasn't any physical possibility that the guy was going to get through that slap without a broken nose. Yet his nose was fine.

Carl imagined that his nose bent in the same way, and as his head rung from the force of the slap, he gingerly explored his nose with a few fingers. He was delighted that nothing was broken.

"Are you paying attention now Carl?" the girl asked.

"Yes." he said with an ounce of indignation. "You didn't have to slap me."

"Yes I did, Carl. I did need to slap you. You gotta hear what I'm telling you, big guy, because I need you. I need you something fierce."

"What are you talking about?"

"You are going to help save a soul today, Officer Carl Friendly." She paused a moment before saying, "I'll let that sink in just a bit."

"Now wait a minute!" Carl jumped to his feet and started backing away.

"Carl Friendly," she said. But it wasn't her voice. "I come to you in your darkest hour." She hadn't even opened her mouth. It was as if James Earl Jones spoke to him in his head. Yet, he knew it came from the girl.

"What's going on?" Carl clutched his head and fell to his knees.

"I have a task for you Carl Friendly." The girl came over to him and held his head in her hands as she stared into his eyes. She was surrounded by light. All he could see was her. All he could hear was her. She was all there was.

"A task?"

"You have been found worthy, Carl Friendly. You have been chosen. If you do as I ask, you may be able to save the lives of five people today. If you do as I ask, you will rid the world of a great evil. It is a terrible burden I place upon you, Carl Friendly, for you may have to sacrifice your own life to save that of another. Will you take up this great burden, Carl Friendly?"

"Yes," he spoke in barely a whisper. "I will take up this great burden for you."

As the words left his mouth, the glow around the girl vanished. Carl no longer felt her presence in his head. And he could once again hear the world around him.

"Good," she said with her own voice. And still holding his head in her hands, she leaned in and kissed him on the forehead. "Good luck, Carl Friendly. And remember that I love you."

And then she was gone.

CHAPTER
TWENTY-FIVE

THE BEAST WOKE TO someone slapping him lightly on his left check. His rage began to build as he opened his eyes, looking for his adversary. Searching for his next fight. But when he gazed out at the world around him, his vision was not clouded by war or aggression or blood or battle. He saw only beauty.

At first he thought that he had come to in the field of yellow roses from his dream. His rage evaporated and was replaced by joy, pure and simple. He had found that which he truly sought. That which was his heart's desire.

He quickly learned that it was not the yellow of the roses he saw above him, but instead was the color of his love's hair.

He blinked.

"Welcome back," she said. Goldilocks smiled as she leaned over him. The Beast could see in her eyes that the smile was genuine. That she was happy to see him. So he smiled back. And for a moment he was swept into the past and was no longer the Beast. He was just Tim. He loved Goldilocks and Goldilocks loved him.

His joy turned to rapture.

He let the past wash over him. He didn't want to let it go. He thought that he might be floating a few hundred feet off the ground, but then decided that he was just really, really happy. He wanted the feeling to last forever. He yearned for it. Ached for it. He needed it. He needed her. And now he had her. Best of all, it appeared that she was happy to see him.

So he flew. He flew higher then he'd been in a long time. He flew so high that he felt he could reach out and touch the sky. He was complete once again.

But then he slammed into something. A barrier. A solid force between him and that which he sought: True happiness, true love, and Goldilocks.

The barrier was a memory. A memory of something he had heard just before he passed out. A memory that had burrowed into his brain like a maggot into rancid beef. A memory that took away his joy. A memory that he didn't want to have, but did.

And so he fell, crashing to Earth and engulfed in flames. Reality reached through the façade that had been built by his true love's smile. Reality reached through the façade and punched him square in the eye. He tried to deny it. Tried to erase the blasted thought from him mind, but it was too late. The thought was planted, and its roots were digging deeper with every passing second.

He frowned up at Goldilocks, and her smile faltered, turning into a look of confusion.

"You're married."

Goldilocks looked away for a moment. A look of guilt mixed with a pinch of shame crossed her face as she said, "Yes. Once. A long time ago."

"A long time ago? But, you're still married?"

"Technically."

"Technically? What's that mean?"

Goldilocks, who still leaned over the Beast, sat back. "It means that on paper, yes, we're still married. Legally speaking."

"Legally speaking?" he sat up. He noticed that the bears had walked a short distance away, giving the two a little privacy.

"I may be married to him in the legal sense," she said. "But I divorced him in my heart years ago."

"Okay, so why not get a legal divorce then? Why stay married to him all this time?"

"It's not that simple."

"Sure it is."

"No," her voice raised in anger. "It isn't."

"Explain it to me then. Explain to me how you could spend all that time with me, pretending to love me, pretending to care. Lying to me the entire time. Good Lord, Golds ... we got married. But that was a lie too!"

"I didn't lie to you."

"You didn't tell me you were married."

"You didn't ask."

"Seriously? That's what you're going with? I didn't ask?"

"I was scared, okay!" Goldilocks stood, wrapping her arms around herself and turning her back on him.

He rose and stood behind her. "Scared of what?"

She turned and looked up into his eyes. "Scared that you wouldn't want to be with me if you knew the truth."

"I'm here, aren't I? Talk to me. What's the truth? Who is this guy?"

"I was young and naive when I met him," she said. "I was just out of school. He was a musician."

"Oh, please," he rolled his eyes.

"Do you want me to tell you the story or not?"

"Okay, I'm sorry."

"He spoke to me, I mean, really spoke to me. He knew just how to get inside my head. How to make me care. He said all the right things. Made all the right moves. But he was a liar. He was a wolf in sheep's clothing. He was a monster. He lied and put on a show and I fell for it." She started to cry. "I fell for all of it."

The Beast took a chance and pulled her into his arms. She accepted and fell into him. He held her as she cried.

"Oh, Lucy!" a voice called distantly from below. The voice of a man calling his dog in for supper. "Here Lucy-Lucy-Lucy! Where are you?"

Goldilocks froze. "It's him. It's Doc." She started to tremble in the Beast's arms.

"Hey," he said, trying his best to sooth her. "It's okay. Who's Lucy?"

"No it's not!" She started to struggle against him. Tried to break free. "It's Doc. He's here! He's going to hurt me again!"

"I won't let that happen. Who's Lucy?"

"You don't know him like I do. We need to hide!"

At that, the big male bear walked over.

"Look," the bear said to the two of them. "I don't know what's going on between the two of you, and I hate to interrupt, but if you're looking to hide, we happen to be in the right place." He pointed to the giant door at the end of the hallway.

"What's behind that door?" the Beast asked, his question to Goldilocks forgotten by the curiosity of the door.

"Come on," the bear said. "I'll show you."

The three walked toward the door. The other two bears were already there, waiting.

"I'm Burt, by the way," the bear said, offering his hand.

"I'm the Beast – well, Tim," he said, shaking Burt's hand.

Burt introduced Tim to his wife and son, then punched a code into the keypad on the wall next to the door.

There was a loud clank from within the wall as the lock disengaged and the door swung outward a couple of inches. The door was all steel, as was the jamb and wall around it. The door reminded Tim of the door to a bank vault. Burt reached in and pulled the door open just enough to allow the five of them to enter the room beyond.

The room beyond the door was actually quite small and sparse. There were two beds, a table and chairs, a few shelves full of canned goods and bottled water, and a computer with a bank of monitors. The monitors showed off various areas in and around the house.

"This is our panic room," Burt said as the door shut behind them.

The locks engaged with a sense of finality that Tim found a little suffocating.

"What do you think?" Burt asked.

"Well," Tim looked around and smiled. He didn't know what he had expected to find, but a cramped room wasn't it. "A little anticlimactic, actually."

CHAPTER
TWENTY-SIX

O FFICER CARL FRIENDLY APPROACHED Griswold House with a mixture of feelings that, taken as a whole, could easily be described as 'having the creeps.'

He checked his weapons one last time as he stood looking into the house from the stoop. Normally, Carl mused, he wouldn't have been able to see into the house from the stoop, but the fact that the door, and about two feet around it, had been blown completely away, it wasn't much of a chore to look in. He sighed, resigned himself to his task, pumped a shell into the shotgun, and stepped into the house.

It was like stepping into Hell.

The quiet slumber of the outside had been replaced by the screams of a million voices. The warm spring air turned to the scorching heat of a colossal oven. The interior décor of the house remained, but everything was either on fire or crawling with maggots, cockroaches, or spiders. The smell in the house was that of old meat and a dead elephant's digestive tract.

Once inside, all five of his senses were treated like the equivalent of a back alley mugging. They were beaten and left for dead.

He back-peddled, almost running backwards out of the doorway behind him and onto the stoop. Carl tripped and fell back on to his bottom, and to his complete embarrassment, fired a round from the shotgun into the wall of the house, a few feet above the gaping hole in the wall where the front door once stood.

Carl rose and found that he was crying, tears rolling down his cheeks like they were fleeing in terror from his body. He couldn't do this. It was too much. He hadn't even made it through the first few steps into the house.

He turned and walked away. He decided to give up on the whole thing. It suddenly struck him that he'd much rather be at home with his dog, Max.

Max was a great big black Labrador with nothing but love for Carl. Max needed Carl. What was he doing here, getting into someone else's business?

He had made it to the end of the drive before he stopped himself. The spot on his forehead, where the little girl had kissed him, began to radiate with warmth. A warmth that he found comforting. He turned back and had just taken a step toward the house when a voice spoke in his mind.

"Where you going, boy?" the voice asked. It was the man in black.

"I'm going into that house," Carl said aloud as he took another step.

"No, son. You don't want to do that."

"Why not?" Carl took another step.

"Well, you might go and get yourself killed. You want to die?"

"No. Of course not."

"Of course not. So why don't you just turn on around and go home to your dog."

"I can't do that," Carl said, taking another step.

"And why is that?"

"I'm supposed to stop you."

The man in black laughed inside Carl's head. "Stop me? Boy, you sure are a funny one. What makes you think that a hick cop like you can stop someone like me?"

"You do."

"Me?" the man in black laughed again. "Son, do you have any idea who am I?"

"No, not really. But I know that you don't want me in that house. That tells me that you're afraid; afraid of me, and of what I might do."

"Afraid!" the man in black laughed some more as Carl moved closer and closer to the house. "Son, you really are a dumb kid. You know that? I have power. Real power. You've see what I can do."

"Yeah, I've seen it. I've seen you kill my friends."

"Then just what is that you think *you're* gonna do, son?" the man in black chuckled.

"That's easy," Carl said as he stepped up onto the stoop. "I'm going to come in there. I'm going to find you. And then I'm going to kill you."

The man in black was silent.

Carl touched his forehead. "Give me the strength," he prayed.

The duffel full of ammunition hung heavily on Carl's right shoulder as he stepped back into Griswold House.

Hell had been replaced by modest furnishings that contrasted with the lavishness of the home's sprawling size. Carl had never been inside Griswold House before today and expected a dwelling of such grand proportions and magnitude to be filled with only the most expensive treasures, the rarest of art, and the finest in technological achievement. And while he did find some of this as he stepped over the threshold and into the front room of Griswold House, he found it to be subtle and sparse instead of garish and in your face.

Carl moved deeper into the house,

It wasn't long before he began to pick up the familiar scent of smoke in the air. He sniffed, tasting the scent, looking about him for any hint of fire. Yet – he sniffed again – this wasn't the kind of smoke that came from fire. Not a house fire anyway, this wasn't wood smoke. Nor was it the smoke of a cigarette, cigar, or any other tobacco. No, there was something dark in this scent. Fire and brimstone. Unholy. Like the fires in the very forges of Hell itself. He didn't like it. He didn't like it one bit. But that's why he was here, right?

Carl pumped a round into the shotgun and continued further into the house, seeking out the origin of the unholy stench. It didn't take long. Carl stepped into a room so full of books that it had to be the library. Shelves that stretched to the ceiling lined the walls.

Carl had never seen so many books outside of a Barnes and Noble. He wanted to stay and browse through the collection, but he didn't stop ... or at least, he hadn't planned on stopping. He was somewhat forced to halt when the owner of the smoky stench strode into the library from the opposite door.

It wasn't at all human. Carl could see this by the way the creature's curled black horns scrapped along the ten foot high ceilings. It was blood red and covered in fur. The smell of brimstone and rot emanated from the twin plumes of smoke that rolled slowly from the thing's nostrils which were perched unnaturally at the end of its wide, squat snout. Long dark teeth protruded upwards from the creature's massive under bite. It held twin swords in arms that were thick with muscle and were bigger than Carl's torso. Its goat legs ended in coal black hooves. Its only adornment was a small gold pendant, a circle of gold, which hung around the thing's neck on a leather cord. Carl began to sweat from the heat that rolled off of the monstrosity in waves.

"You must be Officer Friendly," the thing spoke in a voice so deep and menacing that it put Darth Vader to shame.

"What gave it away," Carl said in a clear, unwavering voice, his confidence surprising even himself. "The police uniform with the name patch?" Carl gestured with his chin toward the patch that said 'Friendly' sewn just above the left breast pocket.

"Sarcasm," it said. "Nice."

"I need you to move."

"I can't do that, meat. I have my instructions. You aren't to pass."

"Well," Carl looked around nervously. "Maybe I'll just back on out of here and take another route."

"Sorry, meat. I can't allow that either."

"Well, *I* can't allow you to keep me here."

"Look, it's really simple," the thing said. "I'm to keep you here in this room. You try and leave and I will kill you, and I won't do it quickly. And believe you me, if there's one thing I know about, it's killing people. The name's Ed, by the way."

Carl shot Ed in the face.

CHAPTER
TWENTY-SEVEN

WE CAN KEEP AN eye on pretty much everything that's going on throughout and around the house from this room," Burt said as he showed Lucy and Tim around the panic room. The tour lasted about thirty seconds and ended with the computer and its bank of monitors.

At the end of the tour, Lucy realized how tired she was. She couldn't remember the last time she had slept.

She glanced over at the beds in the back of the room. They were currently unoccupied. Beatrice and Danny sat at the table putting a puzzle together, and Burt and Tim continued to scrutinize the security monitors. So Lucy made her way over to the beds, hoping to get the chance to take a little nap.

There were two beds total. A toddler-sized bed – a *bear-sized* toddler bed, and a large queen-sized bed. The toddler bed looked just the right size for Lucy so she gave it a try. But like most toddler beds, this one was nothing more than a metal frame and thin mattress. It was just a bit too uncomfortable.

The queen sized bed looked nice and plump, so Lucy climbed up onto one side, lay down, and to her disappointment, found it to be a little too soft. She was about to give up on the idea of sleep when she noticed that this bed wasn't a typical bed. This bed was a Sleep Number bed. So she rolled over to the other side and gave it a try. She sighed with content. It was just right. She wasn't sure who this side was made for, Burt or Beatrice, but Lucy realized that she had just found her Sleep Number.

She closed her eyes and let her mind drift. It wasn't long before sleep tracked her down and threw a dark bag over her head, shutting out the rest of the world.

She entered the world of dreams where she did the kinds of activities she was never able to do in real life. She flew under her own power. She swam the depths of the oceans with no breathing apparatus. She made a goulash that most found quite tasty. She climbed Mount Rushmore and picked George Washington's nose. She saw it all and she did it all. Then, at last, she woke, feeling rested and content.

She sat up in bed and looked over at the clock on the wall. She'd only been sleeping for about five minutes. She sighed, stretched, yawned, and got out of bed to join Beatrice and Danny at the table. It looked like they had finished the puzzle that they had originally started with before Lucy took her nap, and were now deep into another one.

"Would you mind a little help?" Lucy asked, sitting at the table.

"Well," Beatrice said, smiling. "That's up to Danny, he's the puzzle master."

Danny seemed to be ignoring both of them as he picked up pieces and fit them together with nothing more than a quick look over the table with each piece.

"What do you say, Danny?" Lucy asked. "May I join in?"

"Sure," Danny said enthusiastically without looking up.

Lucy studied the pile of puzzle pieces, realizing quickly that they all looked alike to her. She was about to give up when Tim walked up to the table.

"Can I talk to you for a moment?" He asked Lucy.

"Sure," she said, rising. "Sorry I wasn't much help, Danny."

"That's okay," Danny said, still not looking up. "You tried, and that's all that matters."

Beatrice smiled with pride and ruffled the fur on top of Danny's head. She looked up at Lucy and directed the smile at her.

"He's a good kid," Lucy said.

"He's the best," Beatrice replied.

Lucy followed Tim over to the closed door. Tim took her right hand in his and spoke.

"Who's Lucy?"

Well crap, she thought, but aloud she said, "I am. That's my real name."

"Your real name?" Tim looked hurt. "What else have you been hiding from me, Golds?"

Golds, his pet name for her.

"Just that, Tim."

"Just that. Just your real name and your marriage. Those were the only two things you hid from me?"

179

"Well, you already know about my hair."

Tim smiled, "You can't be together as long as we have and not know that one of us has been bleaching their hair. And I knew it wasn't me."

"I guess not," she smiled too.

"But, come on, Golds. Your real name? Your marriage? Those are two pretty big things to hide from someone. Especially someone you claim to love."

"I do love you, but-"

She had to stop talking. It wasn't guilt that made her stop. Or fear. Or even anger. No, it was none of those things. Her reason for stopping mid-sentence was simple. She couldn't talk because Tim was kissing her.

The kiss seemed to last for days – but was actually about twenty seconds – and when it finished, Lucy felt a little weak in the knees.

"That's all I needed to hear from you," Tim said, holding her face in his hands and smiling.

Lucy smiled back, and the two just stood there for a while, looking into each other's eyes and grinning like idiots. An observer would assume the two were drunk, and the observer wouldn't be completely wrong. The two were drunk. They were quite intoxicated. But not from imbibing alcohol. Tim and Lucy were drunk on each other.

And so they started kissing again, quite oblivious to the three bears they currently occupied the small room with. Regardless of the stares, which turned into the loud and obvious clearing of throats, which came from both Burt and Beatrice, the two remained sealed at the lips.

Finally, Burt had to come over and physically separate the two.

Lucy and Tim both stammered a red faced apology, but they still couldn't keep their eyes off each other.

Suddenly, from the bank of security monitors, Beatrice said the only thing that could have pulled Lucy from her spell, "Is this your husband?"

"What?" Lucy asked, spinning in Beatrice's direction.

"Well," Beatrice began. "I just came over to look into the security monitors and I'm seeing this man standing in our kitchen. He's all in black. Is this your husband?"

Lucy and Tim rushed over to the monitor, and there he was. Doc Holliday. Dressed all in black and sporting two antique revolvers. A coldness crept into Lucy and she had to fight to stay on her feet.

Here was the man she'd been running from for the past few years, and he was in the house. Tears leaked from her eyes as she began to tremble. Tim put his arms around her, and while that helped, she still felt a cold stab of darkness in her heart.

Suddenly Doc was looking into the camera. No, looking through the camera.

"He can see me," Lucy whispered. "He knows where I am."

"Now that's just nonsense," Beatrice said.

But then the feed for the camera in the kitchen went out, and the four of them could see nothing now but snow and static coming from the monitor.

"He knows where I am," Lucy repeated. "He knows where I am, and he's going to take me."

"No one's taking you," Tim said.

"He's coming to get me," said Lucy, her voice barely a whisper. "He's coming to get me."

Then the world fell out from under them.

CHAPTER TWENTY-EIGHT

CARL DROPPED THE DUFFEL to the floor before pumping another round into the shotgun as the demon named Ed picked itself up off the floor. The demon was shaken. Carl was sure the thing hadn't expected to be shot in the face, trusting that its demonic presence alone would place such fear in people that fighting back wasn't usually the typical response.

"Okay," the creature laughed. "I'll give ya that one. You got spunk, kid. I won't deny it." Small trails of blood, the deepest of black, oozed from the holes in Ed's face where the blast had taken him.

It bleeds, Carl thought. *That's something.*

"Now, why don't you put the toy down," Ed used the sword in his right hand – a sword so large that Carl could have slept on it –

to gesture at Carl's shotgun. "You're only going to get yourself hurt.

Carl shot Ed in the face.

Once again, Ed fell, this time with a grunt of pain. Carl ran to where Ed lay on the floor, stood over the massive red creature, and continued to pump round after round into the creature's face and head until the the shotgun was out. Carl dropped the shotgun and went for his side arm. By this time, Ed had dropped both swords and had brought his hands up to protect his face. Carl emptied all thirteen rounds from the handgun into the thing's head. Ed stopped moving.

Carl staggered back, breathing heavily, ejecting the empty magazine from the pistol, snatching a fresh one from his his belt, and slamming it into place before returning the Glock 21 to the holder at his hip. He snatched up his shotgun and went to the duffel, crouching and pulling a box of shells from the bag's interior. He slid the last of the eight shells into place when Ed's voice sounded from behind him.

"You finished?"

Carl stood, spun and, pumping a round into the shotgun, pointed the barrel at Ed's mangled face.

"Whoa, there fella," Ed spoke, one hand toying with the gold circlet that hung from the leather cord around its neck, the other hand reaching out in a gesture of peace. Carl wasn't buying it.

Carl shot Ed in the face ... at least, that's what he had meant to do. He had aimed for Ed's face, he had squeezed the trigger, but the shot went wild and blasted the ceiling above. It must have had something to do with Ed moving at the speed of thought and crossing the room to grasp the barrel of the gun with one dinner plate sized hand and pointing said barrel up into the air as Carl fired.

"That's enough!" the demon barked, reaching out with the other had to grab Carl by the top of his head.

Carl felt himself rise from the floor, pain shooting through his head, down his neck, and into his spine. Instinctively, he dropped the shotgun and brought both hands up to grab Ed by the wrist, taking some of his weight off of his head and neck. It still hurt like crap, but luckily the agony didn't last long. Unfortunately, the reason the pain in his spine went away was due to Ed tossing him bodily across the room like an unwanted G.I. Joe action figure. The one pain was replaced by another, an allover agonizing hurt as Carl collided, back first, with a bookshelf on the far side of the room. He slammed to the floor, landing on his chest and face, books from the shelf above falling atop him, the corners of the hardbacks digging into him as they fell. Carl thought for a moment that he was screaming as he flew through the air, he certainly heard someone screaming, but to him it had sounded like a little girl. He supposed it may have been him, but frankly he just didn't care. He simply hurt too much.

"Stay down, hero," Ed said, his voice moving closer. Carl could see its goat's hooves crossing the floor toward him.

"*You* stay down," Carl said, trying for a bit of sass as he struggled to rise. He didn't quite achieve the sass he had been aiming for however. His words came out in a faint croak. He fought with limbs that dared to disobey him, but eventually he began to pull himself up.

"Come on, kid," Ed said, scratching at his chin. "You understand that it ain't gonna mean much to me to kill you, right?"

"*You* come on," Carl, trying for sass again, paused to spit a glob of blood to the floor, "kid." He really hurt. He'd never hurt this bad in his life. The human body just simply wasn't made to be flung about like a toy. He imagined that he had one large bruise that covered every inch of skin on his body.

"Okay, son," the thing spoke as it bent to retrieve one of the massive swords. "Don't say I didn't give you a chance."

Carl knew that he was a dead man. The pain that coursed throughout his body was nothing compared to the hurt in his heart, the pain he felt for failing. Failing her. He had only two options left to him. Run, or stand and fight. He figured that either option led to a horribly unnatural death. Carl made his decision. He made the sign of the cross and launched himself at Ed.

Ed fell back in surprise as Carl slammed into him, wrapping his arms around the thing, clinging to the demon with his feet dangling in the air, fighting the urge to let go from the heat that burned Carl as he came in contact with the creature. But Carl didn't let go. Instead, he slammed his forehead into the thing's snout.

Ed roared and shook Carl free. Carl dropped to the ground and began pummeling the creature, and to his amazement, Ed just stood there and took it. Carl thought for a moment as he danced and punched and kicked that the demon was probably just toying with him. Letting him feel like he was doing well before the red jerk reached out and ended his life like blowing out the candles on a birthday cake. It didn't really matter. Carl was ready to die.

He soon found himself behind the large demon and seized upon the chance, leaping upon the thing's back, wrapping an arm around the creature's throat. Then, grasping his wrist with the other hand to gain leverage, Carl began to choke the life out of Ed, the demon that the man in black had put in his path.

Ed began to take the situation a bit more seriously at that point and managed to get a hand behind its back and grabbed a hold of Carl by the torso. Ed pulled. Carl clung with all his might. But Carl was really no match for the demon's strength and soon felt that if he held on much longer, that the creature would simply pull his arms from their sockets. So Carl let go.

However, as Ed began to pull Carl away, Carl's baser instincts kicked in, his will to live went into overdrive, and his hands and arms flailed about, trying to cling to Ed's shoulders, its neck, its chest. For a moment, his fingers found the leather cord that held the circlet of gold, the cord that hung around Ed's thick neck. Carl snatched at it as Ed gave one last heave.

The cord snapped, and the necklace came off in his hand. He held on to the necklace for dear life and the demon began to scream as it threw Carl across the room

He fell to the floor in a heap, landing on his back, looking up at the demon as it continued to scream. Cracks began to form all over the thing's body, and as they grew larger – widening – smoke roiled forth and he could see inside the demon. It was like looking into a live volcano. Red hot magma began to ooze from the cracks as they continued to open and grow larger.

It took a moment before Carl had realized that the thing had stopped screaming. Instead, the demon trashed about; smoke, flames, and lava pouring out of its body. Then as sudden as it began, it was over. Ed stood frozen. One moment the demon flailed about violently, the next it was as still as a statue. In fact, Carl could see, Ed was a statue. The blood red hue of its skin replaced by that of stone. Smoke no longer rose, fire no longer burned, and lava no longer flowed. Instead, steam emanated from the stone body in great waves as the stone began to cool.

Carl picked himself up off the ground, his clothes torn, his body bloody and bruised, his bones aching. He crossed the room, retrieved his shotgun, pumped a round into the chamber, and shot the statue that was once a demon named Ed. Now it was only pieces of flaky stone as it shattered, scattering around on the library floor.

I'll come back later with a broom and dustpan, Carl thought, snatching up the duffel and striding from the room.

He continued to move forward, but didn't make it far. Something made him stop. He stood in a long hallway with art on the walls. He should continue on, but a small voice inside him told him to go back. He recognized the voice ... the little girl. Carl didn't question it, he just turned on his heel and went back. The girl wanted him to go back to the beginning so that's just where he would go.

CHAPTER TWENTY-NINE

THERE ARE MANY WORDS in the English language that one could use to accurately describe the mood in which Doc Holliday currently found himself in. Irate, furious, even irked would suffice. But in the end, it didn't really matter which word you used, it all came down to the same thing. Doc Holliday was pissed.

He just wanted the girl. He wanted Lucy. She needed to be made an example of to any others who dared think to defy him. But the girl was locked behind a foot of concrete and steel. Not that that would necessarily stop Doc from getting the job done, it just made it more difficult. It meant that he had to expend more energy – use more magic – and he didn't want to have to do that unless it was absolutely necessary.

Doc had spent enough dark energy just to get to this backwater hole. Then there were the cops outside that gas station, plus all those people out front. And now he had this do-gooder lawman creeping about. Officer Friendly. Friendly somehow survived the explosion at the gas station. That made him nervous, and Doc didn't get nervous.

So he had used more of his power to try and drive Friendly away. He had tried an all-out assault on the boy's senses. That almost worked, but the boy persisted. Then he had tried persuasion. That nearly worked as well. But the boy was still able to follow him into the house. He didn't have much time. That meant using even more energy. He'd sent Ed, one of his minions from the Pit, to keep Carl from interfering. But now he no longer sensed Ed's presence on Earth. There was no way that boy got past Ed. Yet ... he tried not to think about it.

Focus on the plan, he thought. *Focus on Lucy. Get Lucy. Go home. Simple.*

Doc may seem all powerful to the useless human carrion that infested the planet, but the fact of the matter was that his power was not infinite. Not even close. Oh, he had ways of getting back that which he had used, but it involved a full moon, goat skin leggings, and the blood of a virgin. Three things he didn't have immediately at hand.

There *was* one other option available to him, but he wasn't too keen on it. He'd never had to use it before, and he wasn't about to start. It meant calling upon his boss, facing him, and then asking for a favor. He already owed the Boss as it was, and he didn't like being beholden to anyone, leastways the Devil himself. But knowing that the option was there – just in case – helped ease his tension just a little.

As it sat now, he didn't have much of the dark energy left in him. Just enough to get in, get the girl, and get out. He would to have to rely on shock and awe. He needed to go in fast, expend a nice big chunk of power, blow some stuff up, put stars in their eyes, grab the girl, and then get the Hell out of Dodge.

He found himself in a room on the first floor, and he stood looking up at the ceiling. Above him, two floors directly above him, was the panic room. In the panic room was his prize. Lucy. The rest, the bears and that boy who calls himself the Beast, they were nothing more than cattle for the slaughter. But only if they got in his way. Doc didn't have the time, nor the energy, for a drawn out battle.

The panic room was heavy, real heavy, but the walls around him were made up of steel support beams behind dry wall which held the panic room in place. He just needed to knock out those support beams and the room would come tumbling down. Then it was a just a simple matter of getting into the room and absconding with the girl.

He mentally checked his power levels. He would have to melt steel, twice, then he should have just enough power left to teleport a short distance. Teleporting took quite a bit of raw energy, otherwise he'd just teleport into the room, grab Lucy, and teleport out. But he only had enough in him for one jump. So he would melt his way in instead. Dropping the room down two floors should shake them up enough that he'd be a couple of blocks away before the rest of them would even know what happened.

Doc pulled his guns. Through them he was able to direct the Hellfire he had at his disposal. He aimed at the wall to his left with one pistol, and the wall to his right with the other. He squeezed the triggers. A bar of molten fire, as thick as the barrel of each gun, shot forth from both revolvers and melted through the wall at either side. Then he spun a full circle, once, as the fire shot from his guns, and the house started to rumble.

Doc casually stepped through the doorway and into the next room as Lucy, her friends, and the steel box they were hiding in came crashing down through the floor in a cloud of dust, splintered wood, and sparking electrical wires. He smiled at the sight of the ruin he had caused. He loved ruin. Ruin, chaos, anarchy – these were his bread and butter.

The room sat at an angle, resting on one corner. Before the dust could settle, he raised his right pistol and traced a bar of Hellfire in a circle – big enough for a man to fit through – on one side of the giant steel box. The circle complete, he kicked at it and it fell inward, into the panic room, leaving a nice hole in the wall that Doc stepped through.

Inside the room Doc found a chaotic mess. Everything in the room that wasn't bolted down had slid to the downward pointing corner of the box. The occupants inside were dazed and lying on the floor. He located Lucy lying next to the Beast. She looked up at him in confusion. The confusion turned into recognition, which then changed to terror.

"Hello, Lucy," he said as he picked her up and threw her over a shoulder.

She screamed and hit at him, clawing and kicking. He just laughed.

And just as he was about to teleport away, he looked down and gazed upon the Beast – the man whom Lucy truly loved. The

Beast was handsome, he could see that. But he was still just a man, after all.

Doc teleported. His destination had been the smoldering parking lot of the Brick House Gas and Groceries just down the road. But that's not where he ended up. Instead, he found himself still in the house. He stood in the front room. The front door, or the gaping hole in the wall that had replaced it, was there in front of him.

To make matters worse, standing between Doc and the outside was that blasted do-gooder cop, Officer Carl Friendly. He'd gotten past the demon. Doc couldn't believe it.

"Howdy Doc," the boy said, pumping a round into the shotgun he held. "I'm going to need you to lay the girl on the ground and throw your hands in the air."

Doc felt a surge of rage build up inside him. He was Doc Holliday. There was a time when the name alone would turn a man's insides to jelly, yet here was this law man, this *boy*, presuming to tell him what to do. It was preposterous, ridiculous, and frankly, a little offensive. But he was practically out of juice. A sliver of fear began to creep in. He fought it back, pushing it off into another room and locking the door.

Doc shifted Lucy around on his shoulder, trying to make himself more comfortable as Officer Friendly continued to point the shotgun at him. He had to end this quick. What should have been a simply snatch and grab had turned out to be more than he had bargained for and he wasn't sure if he had the power left to dispose of any of these people in the fashion to which he'd gotten used to. But he wasn't worried. After all, he was still Doc Holliday, powers or not. He still had the skills required to take out one little law man. Besides, you'd have to be a sand blasted idiot to fire off a shotgun at someone holding the person you were trying to protect. Shotguns were just not made for precision shooting.

So, instead of doing what the nice officer had asked, and put the lady down, Doc kept her right where she was at, and drew one of his pistols. He smiled as he pointed it at Officer Friendly.

"Come on, Carl," he said, thumbing back the hammer. "You and I both know that you ain't gonna shoot me with that scatter gun. Not when I got this pretty lady here on my shoulder."

"No?" Carl said.

"No."

"You're fairly certain of that, are you?"

"I am," Doc said as he thought, *the nerve of this boy*. "Now be a good boy, and put your gun down. And then, while you're at it and just to keep things orderly and ironic, you can go and thrown your own dern hands in the air."

But the boy didn't drop the gun, and he most certainly did not throw his dern hands in the air. No, instead, Officer Carl Friendly did the one thing that Doc did not expect. The boy threw the shotgun into Doc's face and ran for it.

Doc was, of course, somewhat surprised to have a large metal object hurled into his face, and so he did what most would do. His face scrunched up and his eyelids fluttered in that way that they do when you expect something big, heavy, and painful to slam into your face, something you just know is going to hurt like the almighty dickens. While this was happening, he also brought his hands up to cover his face. Not to hide the look his face was making, which *would* be quite embarrassing if anyone saw it, but more to protect his delicate facial features from the shotgun that was about to smash into them. This then caused two things to happen.

One, his right hand – the one holding the pistol – clenched for a moment as it rose to cover his face. And, as he had a finger on the trigger, the pistol fired. Which in turned caused him to jump slightly, relax his hold on the gun, and drop it.

Two, his left hand – the one that held Lucy – discontinued its task and rose to cover his face. So, as the gun went off in his right hand, and he jumped slightly, Lucy slid off of his left shoulder and fell onto the floor.

The sound – combined with the sudden flight to the floor – caused Lucy to scream, which in turn caused him some minor irritation, but not as much as the shotgun to the face.

All in all, only a few seconds went by from the time the shotgun left Carl's hand to the time it hit the floor, but when Doc pulled his hands from his face, Carl was gone. Not completely however. He spied the back of one of Carl's feet as it disappeared through the giant hole in the wall that used to be the front door.

So he crouched, grabbed the fallen pistol in his right hand, and one of Lucy's ankles with the left. Then he stood and walked calmly out of the hole and into the front yard, dragging Lucy behind him.

Outside he was met by a crowd of people. It was like the whole dern town had turned out for the show. But it wasn't just the townsfolk. The State Police had arrived. They had already taped off the whole area and were now keeping people back, shouting "Nothing to see here", and generally going through the motions. Doc could see that they didn't have any real idea just what was going on here, but they were doing what they could.

Well, he would just have to show them *all* what was really going on.

He lifted his six shooter, thumbed back the hammer, and shot Carl Friendly in the right leg as the boy ran toward the State Police and their tape barrier. Carl had barely made it to the halfway point when he went down with a shout of pain.

It took a moment for the people and the Staties to react. About as long as it took for the sound of the gunshot to dissipate. By then, Doc had dragged a struggling Lucy across the lawn to the prone form of Carl Friendly. There he let go of her ankle, pulled his other pistol, pointed them both in the air, and faced the State Police.

The State Police, by that time, fired up about four spotlights and aimed them in his direction. He supposed they were there to disorientate and blind him, which they did, but he knew that behind the lights were people, and that's really all he needed to know.

"Don't move!" an amplified voice sounded from behind the lights.

He laughed. These people had no idea who they were dealing with. Sure, he had used all of his power, but he still had one card up his sleeve.

Doc Holliday couldn't die.

Well, that wasn't entirely true. He could be shot, he could feel pain, and his body could die. His soul, on the other hand, would just be sent back to Hell. From there the Boss would just place his soul into a different body and send him on back up. He didn't like it. He found the whole process agonizingly painful. But he'd go through it to get out of a tough spot if he needed to.

196

The goal however, was to try as he might to get himself, and the girl, out of here. But he liked having options. Besides, if it really came down to it, he could always call on the Boss to come up and give him a power up. It meant owing the Boss more souls, but Doc was up to the task.

"Drop the weapons!" the amplified voice returned. "Drop the weapons now or we will open fire!"

"Me first," Doc said, and began squeezing off shot after shot, into the lights, laughing as he heard the bullets make contact with flesh.

CHAPTER
THIRTY

TIM – THE BEAST – AWOKE amidst smoke and ruin. He shook his head, trying to clear his mind, trying to recall what had happened. But it was cloudy. Elusive. One moment they had been watching Doc through the security monitor. The next they were falling. That's when the world went black.

All in all, Tim had begun to get rather tired of passing out. He figured that he might want to see a doctor at some point, once this was all over. Passing out as many times as he had in the last few hours couldn't be good for one's physical health or mental well-being.

But he would worry about that later. There were more pressing things at hand.

Tim stood and brushed himself off. He found it difficult to stay on his feet, which had nothing to do with the multiple black outs. No, he couldn't manage to stay balanced because the floor was pitched at a near fifteen degree angle.

He looked around. He saw a giant lump of brown fur that he guessed to be the three bears, but he didn't see Lucy anywhere.

"Lucy?" he called out, the dust in the air making him cough.

No answer.

He noticed a large hole in the wall that hadn't been there before the world dropped out from under them. The steel around the hole looked as if it had been melted through. But what could do that?

"Lucy?" he called again, stumbling around the room. "Where are you, baby?"

The Griswolds began to stir. Burt was the first to his feet, but the other two were quick to follow.

"Lucy!" Tim yelled. Panic had begun to set it.

"What happened, Burt?" Beatrice said as she and Danny clung to her husband.

"We're on the ground floor," Burt said, looking through the hole. "Something brought the entire panic room down."

"What could do that?" Beatrice asked.

Doc, he thought. It didn't make any sense, but it had to be Doc.

Lucy was scared stiff of the man, and he'd never known her to be scared of anything, or anyone. But that man put a fear in her that he had never seen. Doc did this. He didn't know how, but he was certain of the who and the why.

That's what Lucy has been running from all this time. Not Tim. Doc. And Doc had found her. Found her, and took her. And Tim had to get her back.

"Burt?" Beatrice said, looking scared. "What could bring this entire room down through the floor?

"Not what," Tim said, checking his revolver. "Who."

"What?" Burt asked.

"Not what, Daddy. Who." Danny said.

"This man that Lucy was so afraid of," Tim said, ignoring the boy. "Doc. He did this."

"What makes you think that?" Beatrice asked.

"He's taken Lucy," Tim said.

"Now, you don't know that," Burt said.

Tim stepped through the hole in the panic room wall. "Well, she sure isn't here. And I don't think she'd leave." He looked around. "Yeah, he took her."

"Tim, don't be rash." Beatrice said as the Griswolds followed him out of the panic room.

"I agree with Bea," Burt said. "Anyone capable of pulling that room through two floors and then melting a hole through a foot of steel isn't someone to trifle with."

"Neither am I," Tim said, turning to look at Burt. "There's a reason I'm called 'The Beast'. It's time Doc found out why that is."

Just then, from outside, there came a gunshot, followed by a woman screaming.

"Lucy!" Tim shouted, running toward the sound.

The Griswolds followed him as he ran through the house. It wasn't far to the front door and so it wasn't long before he found himself outside.

A crowd had gathered, drawn by the rumor of dirty work afoot. The State Police were on the scene. Crime tape was thrown up in a perimeter around the front lawn of the house. There were people on the other side of the tape, lots of people.

Suddenly he was blinded as the State Police flipped on no less than four spotlights, flooding the front of the house with a white fire that pinned Tim where he was.

"Don't move!" sounded an amplified voice.

For a moment, Tim thought the voice was directed at him, until he noticed Doc just a few dozen yards away. And at the ground at Doc's feet, lay two figures. A man, and Lucy.

The man lay sprawled and unmoving. Lucy lay curled up and crying. Doc just stood, defiant and laughing, his guns raised in apparent triumph and glee.

"Drop the weapons!" the amplified voice returned. "Drop the weapons now or we will open fire!"

But it was Doc who opened fire. Tim couldn't see where Doc aimed as he fired into the light, but he knew the sound of bullets hitting bodies when he heard it. Then Lucy was on her feet and wrestling with Doc. He was about to rush to her side when Doc pushed her from him and slammed her across the face with the barrel of one of his revolvers.

He would never forget the sound that the steel made as it connected with her face, her mouth, her teeth. He would never forget the way she dropped, just dropped, like a marionette that had had its strings cut. He would never forget the way she lay there. Unmoving. Inert. Silent. He would never forget the fury that rose within him.

"You son of a b-!" the rest of the word had been drowned out by the popping of bone as Tim began to grow. To change. To transform.

Where Tim once stood, now stood the Beast in all his glory. At seven feet tall he was nothing more than fur, muscle, teeth, and claws.

Doc turned in time to witness Tim's transformation. Doc only smiled as the Beast pointed at him.

"Now you will know why I am called the Beast!" the thing that was once Tim roared.

The Beast drew his sword and charged.

CHAPTER THIRTY-ONE

DOC HOLLIDAY HAD FACED creatures such as the Beast many times since his resurrection. He wasn't worried. He'd found more often than not that their bark was worse than their bite, especially after you put a .45 caliber slug into their head. So he took aim as the Beast, roaring and slavering – all claws, teeth, and fur – came at him.

Doc fired and the Beast slid out of the way, the bullet sailing harmlessly past as the Beast kept coming. Doc fired a second time, but again the Beast stepped out of the path of the bullet.

Doc managed to get off one more shot before the Beast was on him. This shot too missed and suddenly the Beast was there, swinging the sword.

Doc Holliday had not been idle in the hundred or so years since his resurrection. Sure, he'd been given access to the darkest of magic and his power was great, but Doc had always been a practical man. Using the inexhaustible wealth at his command, Doc had spent much of his time first learning – then mastering – a veritable smorgasbord of martial arts. So as the Beast's sword arched toward his head, Doc dropped both pistols, reached out, took hold of the Beast's wrist, and stepped to the side, spinning and using the Beast's momentum to flip the creature over his shoulder and drive it into the ground.

Doc laughed.

That's when Lucy leaped on him. She bled copiously from the wound on her face where he had struck her with the barrel of his gun. Her blood flew at him in large droplets as she hit and kicked and bit at him, screaming and spitting as if she channeled the very animal rage that had come from the Beast. Doc continued to laugh. He pushed her off of him with ease. And as she lay there on the ground, looking up at him in defiance, blood and tears staining her face, he drove a boot heel into the bridge of her nose. She crumpled.

Suddenly he was knocked off of his feet from behind. He landed on his chest, the wind rushing from his lungs with the impact. He flipped over and looked up into the barrel of a fancy new service pistol held by Carl Friendly.

"Hiya, Doc," Carl said. "Should we try this again?"

But then the Beast was on them, throwing Carl to the side like a child's toy and picking Doc up over its head as if he were made of polystyrene. Before Doc could think clearly, he was soaring through the air, stopping short when he slammed into the side of the house.

Doc was hurt. He was bleeding and broken, and frankly, he'd had enough. As the Beast tore its way to him, running on all fours, grass and dirt flying from its hands and feet, Doc spoke a name. A name that cannot be repeated here, for it is a name of great power and great evil.

At the sound of the name, everything around them ceased to move. Time itself seemed to pause as silence pushed its way in around them. The stillness lasted for only a heartbeat and then the ground between them erupted, knocking them off of their feet. A column of fire, as wide as the Washington Monument shot out of the ground and into the air, high enough to penetrate the clouds and push them aside.

Doc stepped back, holding a hand up to his face to shield it from the heat. The Boss sure liked to make an entrance.

Creatures erupted from the flames. They were all wings and scales, teeth and claws. They flew about around them, screeching and shrieking, sounding like the shouts of pain that come following the most brutal of torture.

The fire died and in its place stood a being of shadow and flames. A creature of darkness and decay. Of lies, deceit, and pure evil. Doc just had to smile. The Boss had arrived.

But at that very instant, as Doc smiled and began to feel triumph, a small girl appeared before the Boss. She was about five or six years old and her chin length brown hair sported six small pigtails around her head. Doc gaped. It shouldn't be. She shouldn't be here. All was lost.

"You," the Boss said.

"Me," the girl said.

Neither of them moved. They only stood, looking each other over. The Boss with a smile of contempt on his face, the girl a smile of confidence.

"It was foolish of you to come, Morning Star," the girl said.

"We shall see who the fool is," the Boss replied. "This does not concern you. Leave now and I will not hurt any of these pets you seem to care so much for."

"You always were impetuous," the girl smiled, "but now you're in my house."

She raised her hand and it all came to an end.

CHAPTER
THIRTY-TWO

BEATRICE BEAR HAD ALWAYS felt that she truly understood fear. She'd felt its icy fingers many times in her life.

When she had married Burt and they had little money, Beatrice feared for their future. When she became pregnant, she feared for the baby inside her. When Danny was diagnosed with autism, she feared for her son and what might be waiting for him when she was gone. Beatrice and fear were old friends.

But until today, the fear that Beatrice had known was fear of the unknown. Fear over an outcome she could not predict. It was a fear she couldn't run and hide from, so she had faced that fear head on.

Today she had learned a different kind of fear. Fear of violence. Fear of pain. Fear of death.

The three bears had been following Tim on his mad dash through the house. When they had reached the front door, or what was left of it, they found chaos on the lawn.

The man in black was there, firing off his guns into a crowd of people. Officer Carl Friendly was there too, and so was Lucy.

Beatrice was afraid for her family. But she was afraid for her new friends too. This man in black, this Doc, looked crazed. Insane. Beatrice wanted to put as much distance between her family and that man as she could.

That's when Tim started to change. Beatrice shrank back as some kind of monster, some kind of beast, took Tim's place and charged into battle.

When the bullets started to fly, Burt put himself between the danger and his family. There are many aspects of her husband that had made Beatrice Bear fall in love with him. His generosity, his loyalty, his sense of humor, and – of course – his dashing good looks. But his instinctual desire to protect his family made her wish at that moment that the two of them were alone so that she could – well, now was not the time to think of such things.

In the meantime, Beatrice could see the conflict arising within Burt. On the one hand he wanted to be there for his family – to keep them safe. On the other hand, Burt could see that his new friends needed help, and he wanted to be out there in the fight. Beatrice was conflicted as well. She wanted Burt to stay. She wanted Burt to sacrifice anything and everyone to ensure that his family was safe. Yet, she knew that Burt could help. She wanted their new friends to survive. She wanted Tim and Lucy to be together. And she knew that Burt had the skills necessary to get the job done.

Beatrice put her hand on Burt's arm. She was about to tell him to go. To help. And to come back in one piece. But she never got the chance. Something – well, Beatrice wasn't quite sure exactly what it was, but a presence was on the lawn. Something dark and twisted. Something evil.

Her hand no longer rested on Burt's arm. Instead, she clutched at it.

That's when the little girl arrived.

Time stood still.

There was no wind. No sound. No smells. No movement. Nothing. Just the complete absence of everything but what Beatrice could see. And what she could see wasn't much.

The little girl just stood there, serene, facing the presence of Evil. This may have gone on for a few seconds. It may have gone on for a few years. Beatrice couldn't be sure. It felt like both, but the passage of time was nonexistent.

And with the same suddenness as they appeared, the little girl and the evil presence were gone and the world exploded back into place around them.

"What happened, Mommy?" Danny began to cry.

She could see the panic in the cub's eyes. This was all too much for her son. Too much stimulation, not enough routine. Her little guy had been holding himself together through it all, but now she could see that he had had enough. He was about to break, to crack, and she knew a meltdown was imminent.

Beatrice tried to comfort her cub, but Danny proved to be difficult.

"I want to go home," he was saying. His voice rising in both volume and pitch.

Then Burt was there, and soon all three were wrapped up in each other as Burt enveloped them for one massive hug.

"I don't like this, Mommy," Danny sobbed into her. "I don't like this at all. I want to go home. I want all these people to go away!"

Burt went down on one knee, looked Danny in the eyes, and held him gently by the shoulders. "It's going to be okay, pal."

"No it won't!" Danny screamed. "You don't get it!" Danny ripped himself free from Burt's hold. "It's never going to be okay again!"

And before Burt or Beatrice could react, Danny started to run. But not away from everything. In his panic, Danny didn't realize that he was running toward the scene on the lawn.

Tim and Carl were struggling with the man in black, who seemed to be going crazy following the disappearance of the little girl and the evil presence.

A shot rang out.

Danny fell.

One moment he was running, then he was down, as if all the life had gone out of him in an instant.

Beatrice screamed, "NO!" and everything stopped.

The world was swept into a silent stillness. Yet Danny still lay there, unmoving, his body in an unnatural position.

Beatrice and Burt ran to their son. Beatrice got there first, fell to her knees, and scooped the cub up into her arms, cradling him, holding him close, rocking gently back and forth, and crying.

"My boy," Burt cried, kneeling down beside Beatrice. "Not my boy!"

Beatrice looked up at her husband. "Why, Burt? Why did this happen?" It didn't make any sense. No sense at all. It couldn't be true. That wasn't blood she felt running down her arms, coming from her son. She wouldn't believe it.

"My son! God no! Not my son!" Burt sobbed, overcome with grief.

"I-I didn't," a voice sounded beside them. "I didn't mean it."

Beatrice looked up. It was the man in black, and he held a pistol. Smoke rolled gently from the barrel.

"I'm sorry," the man in black said as their eyes met. Beatrice could see his confusion, his sorrow, and his guilt in those eyes. "I, didn't … I don't understand what's going on. I don-"

The rest of what he was about to say was drowned out by a roar of pure animal rage.

Burt reached out and took Doc by the throat. He lifted the man from the ground like he was made from straw, holding him high before driving him back to the dirt with the force of a jack hammer.

"Burt, no!" Beatrice screamed.

Burt straddled Doc and made a fist. He drove the fist into Doc's face as the man lay lifelessly on the ground. He rained down blows on Doc Holliday with a rage that Beatrice had never before seen.

Suddenly Officer Friendly was there. He tried to grapple Burt from behind, to pull her husband from the man he was trying to kill, but Burt wouldn't have it. He simply flexed and Carl was thrown from him.

Beatrice fell to her knees and watched helplessly as Burt mercilessly beat the man that had shot her son. It suddenly dawned on her that if she truly wanted to stop her husband from killing the man she could do so. But a hard part deep within her decided that she was fine right where she was.

CHAPTER THIRTY-THREE

L UCY SHRANK BACK IN terror at the sight of Burt as he pummeled the life from her husband. Burt Griswold had truly lost control following the loss of his son, but then ... wouldn't anyone? He had let the animal inside of him out. Lucy truly feared for her life as she bore witness to this most grizzly murder.

Burt raged and roared. He clawed and he bit. Doc Holliday, Lucy's estranged husband, just simply didn't have a chance.

When it was all over, Lucy watched as Burt pulled himself back, his mouth and hands dripping with Doc's life-blood. Burt stumbled over to his wife as she cradled their son. Wiping at his mouth with sleeve, he dropped to his knees, took the two in his arms, and mourned along with his wife.

Then Tim was at her side, no longer the Beast, his clothes torn and ragged. He pulled her into his arms and the two gave Burt and Beatrice the space they needed to comfort each other.

Just then she heard a noise coming from Doc. She pulled away from Tim and moved closer. She was surprised to find that Doc was still alive. He was an awful bloody mess, but he still hung in there. He was muttering something, but she couldn't quite make it out. So she bent closer.

"I'm sorry," Doc said. And for a moment she thought that he had spoken to her, until she saw the look in his eyes. He wasn't looking at her. He looked through her, as if to something behind her. She had begun to turn, to see what it was that Doc was seeing, but something about his eyes made Lucy pause. They weren't the cruel, heartless eyes of her husband. They were soft. They were true, as if the eyes Lucy had always known had never belonged to the man she called her husband. Yet these eyes, these were the man's true eyes.

"I'm s-sorry," Doc repeated, the words sounding like a sheet of paper being drawn across rough concrete. "I can't escape the ... the things I've done. The people I've k-killed."

Doc Holliday went into a coughing fit, blood foaming on his lips.

"Doc," she said. "Don't, don't talk."

But he ignored her like she wasn't even there.

"I did a lot of people a lot of wrong," Doc said. "And all I'm asking for ... all I'm asking for is that you can forgive me." Doc fell into another coughing fit before continuing. "Please forgive me."

That was when his eyes changed. Suddenly they were the eyes she had known for all those years. The hatred, the callous disregard for human life, they showed now once again in Doc's eyes.

He pushed Lucy back from him and began to rise, clutching at his gun. She couldn't move.

"Lucy!" Tim called out from behind.

Doc Holliday stood straight and tall, his face a mask of indifference as he pointed the revolver at her, the barrel finding a point just between her eyes. The man never spoke. He only sneered as he used his thumb to pull the hammer back, readying the gun to end her life.

"I forgive you, Doc," she said, and for a moment, as he put pressure on the trigger, his eyes changed once more. The true eyes.

A shot rang out and Lucy flinched. Doc fell. The shot had not come from his gun. She turned and there stood the ragged and bloody police officer that had tried to save her before, a gun held in his shaky hand. Carl, Doc had called him Carl.

"I'm sorry," the officer said quietly and fell to his knees.

Lucy looked to the limp form of her husband and watched in quiet dispassion as, for the second time in his life, John Henry "Doc" Holliday died.

"I never killed a man before," the officer spoke. She turned and looked at the man as he knelt, cradling his pistol. He didn't appear to notice the bullet wound in his leg. "I've never even fired my gun in the line of duty before today. Not once."

"Carl," she started to say, but suddenly Burt and Beatrice were there, kneeling with Carl, holding him. It was a testament to the bears, how they could turn their own grief into understanding. How they could share that understanding with Carl.

"I wanted him to die," Burt said, choking back a sob. "I needed him to die, for what he did to my boy ... but," Burt stopped, looked around and took a breath, trying not to cry. "But not this way."

"It's okay, Burt," his wife held him tighter.

"But that's not it, Bea," Burt rose in anger. "I wanted the man dead, but *I* wanted to be the one to kill him. Dangit, Bea. I **needed** to kill that man." Lucy could see the big bear struggling to keep the tears back.

"What's wrong with me, Bea? I'm not a cold blooded killer."

Beatrice held him.

"I'm sorry, Bea," Burt said. "I'm sorry about Danny. I'm sorry for what I wanted to do."

The two bears held tightly to each other, rocking back and forth, weeping softly. And suddenly, Tim was there, pulling Lucy close to him.

"I'm the one who killed him," the officer broke the silence, speaking in almost a whisper. She looked over at the man. He stared off into the distance. "I took a man's life today. Regardless of what he had done, regardless of the man he was, I still took his life."

Beatrice reached out and touched him lightly on the shoulder.

"Don't, Carl," she said. "It's not your fault."

"She's right," someone said from behind them. "This is not your fault, Carl Friendly. You didn't kill John Holliday"

They all turned to look and saw a little girl standing there. She was about six with a white star on her shirt and seven pigtails sticking up all over her head.

"You!" Carl shouted.

"Yes, Carl. It is me." The girl smiled.

"But-" Carl began.

"How about we take care of that leg?" the girl said.

She laid a hand on Carl's wound and a blinding light shown from between her fingers. When she took her hand away, his wound had been heeled.

Lucy felt a wave of peace slide over her. The sadness, the grief, the fear ... it was all gone. Something about this little girl just washed it all away.

"But, how can you say that it's not my fault?" Carl asked, oblivious of the miracle that had been performed on his leg. "How can you say I didn't kill him? I killed that man. Me. I shot him. I pointed my gun at him and squeezed the trigger. I knew what I was doing."

"Well, Carl. You couldn't have killed John Holliday. He wasn't really alive," the girl's manner was more teacher than six year old. "And if he wasn't really alive, then you didn't really kill him." She smiled again.

This was greeted with an unbelieving silence from Lucy and her companions.

"I'm sorry," Carl said, wiping the tears from his eyes, "but I don't understand that one bit."

"John Holliday died in Glenwood Springs, over a hundred and twenty years ago. This," she pointed at Doc's body, "was nothing more than a shell. A host for the evil that was placed inside him."

"Evil?" Beatrice asked as they all started to gather around the small girl. "Who would put evil inside of him?"

"Why, the Devil, dear. Who else?" the girl responded.

"The Devil?" Tim laughed. "Now you're talking about Heaven and Hell and God and the Devil. I'm sorry, but I just don't believe in all that."

"That's really too bad, son. Because we all believe in you," the girl said.

"Who are you?" Burt asked.

"I am who I am." The girl replied.

"Are you –" Beatrice paused and cleared her throat. "Are you God?"

"I'm not a big fan of labels," the girl said. "I am who I am. That is all."

"Can you forgive me for killing that man?" Carl asked, pointing at Doc.

"Like I said, Carl. John Holliday wasn't really alive, not in the spiritual sense. So technically, you didn't kill him. Well, you killed his body, yes, but what you really did was set him free."

"Set him free?" Carl asked.

"You see, when John Holliday died way back when, the Devil took his soul to Hell. The Devil then broke John's soul into pieces, leaving just a small fraction of it left within him. Think of a soul like a bag of hammers."

"A bag of hammers?" Tim asked incredulously.

"Okay," the girl continued. "Not a bag of hammers. Think of it like a soft feather pillow. All of the feathers inside that pillow make up your soul. Each time you do something wrong, one of those feathers goes away. Each time you do something to make up for that wrong, another feather comes and takes its place. You follow me so far?"

They all nodded in unison.

"It's actually much more complicated than that, I mean we are talking about a soul after all, but this analogy should help you understand. Okay?"

They all nodded again.

"The Devil, he emptied that pillow of all those feathers. All those feathers but one. See, a person still needs that one small piece of himself to work. The Devil could have emptied the pillow completely, but then John would have just become nothing more than an unthinking automaton. No, the Devil needed John to keep that one last feather. That way the Devil could fill the pillow with pieces of himself. Then the evil would corrupt the last part of John that remained, make John into something he wasn't, and yet the Devil would still have something that could make its own decisions."

The girl stopped for a moment and looked at each one in turn. Making sure that they were all taking everything in. Making sure they understood.

"That evil, think of them as black feathers, those black feathers were what gave John his power. Each time John used his – well, let's just go ahead and call it 'magic'. Each time John used his magic, he'd burn through some of those black feathers. Then he'd have to travel the road to Hell so that the Devil could top off his tank and send him back out into the world again."

"But today, well today John used too much of his dark power. Today John burned through all of those black feathers, and all that remained was that solitary white one. The one the Devil corrupted, but was still a part of who John was. John knew he was out of power, but he couldn't travel the road to Hell. He had to expend power to do that, and he didn't have any left. The only way he could get his boss to fill the tank was to call him up here, to Earth. And the Devil, being rather foolish I must say, came on up. I took that opportunity to fill up John's tank myself."

"Okay, I'm lost again," said Carl. "What does, well, what does Doc's boss being here on Earth have to do with you filling up Doc's tank."

"Well," the girl explained. "Once the Devil had corrupted John's soul, John became a creature of the Devil. I can't just go in and replace all that evil while it's there. I mean, I could, sure ... but we are talking some monumental power here. Continents would have shifted and all that. So I needed John empty. I needed him down to that last feather, the feather that was his own. I also needed to wrestle John's soul from the Devil before I could fill John's pillowcase back up again.

"But with white feathers, this time, right?" Carl asked.

"You get the gold star, Carl. See, in most ways, the Earth is my domain. The Devil has power here, sure. But I did create the place, after all. So yes, I could stride down into the Pits of Hell to grapple with the Devil, but again, a wrestling match of such power, well ... what would have been the purpose to save one man's soul if I destroyed the Earth in the process? So up here, the Devil has less power. Up here I can do what needs to be done without setting the world on fire. So ... I took the opportunity to help set John Holliday free. I sent the Devil packing, topped John off, and left him here with you."

"And then I killed him," said Carl, sullenly.

"Yes you did, Carl. But it needed to be done. When I was finished with John, he was back to being his old self. He didn't recall the last hundred or so odd years he spent here on Earth because he wasn't himself when he lived them. His last memory was of the day he died in Colorado. He was fresh and clean and ready to join me in Heaven."

The girl then put a hand on Carl's shoulder, which to Lucy, shouldn't have been possible, considering that Carl was twice as tall as the girl. Yet she managed it anyway, and without any outward appearance that she was breaking all known laws of physics. Lucy knew it should look odd, but it didn't and so Lucy promptly forgot all about it.

"Don't fret on it Carl," the girl said. "He's not supposed to be alive. He died on November 8th, 1887. He should have been in Heaven over a hundred years ago. You just helped put him where he belonged."

"But, he killed my son." Beatrice said, anger creeping into her voice.

"Did he?" the girl responded.

"Mommy?" Danny's voice sounded behind them. "Daddy?"

CHAPTER
THIRTY-FOUR

BURT STOOD IN DISBELIEF alongside his equally confused wife.

His boy was dead. Danny was dead. He had died. Yet, here he was. Smiling.

"I want some gum," the boy said, causing Burt and his wife to burst into tears. They both dropped to their knees and pulled Danny into a hug.

"Why are you crying?" Danny asked.

Burt and Beatrice just laughed and continued holding on to their little boy. Burt turned his head to look at the girl.

"I don't understand," Burt said. "He was dead."

"He wasn't supposed to die," the little girl replied. "That was not his purpose. He's meant for greater things in this world."

"Thank you," Burt said, tears running down his furry face. "Thank you!"

And that was how it was for a time. Burt and Beatrice, holding tight to their boy, afraid to let go. Neither one daring to speak. Both content to just remain as such for as long as they could. Danny however, had other plans.

"Uh, guys," Danny said from within his parent's embrace. "What about my gum?"

Everyone laughed, including Tim, Lucy, and Carl. Even the little girl giggled just a bit as Beatrice handed Danny a stick of gum.

"Why's everyone looking at me?" Danny asked as he chewed.

And everyone laughed again.

"We're just happy to see you," Beatrice said, hugging Danny close again.

"We sure are," said Lucy, drawing close to Tim as he wrapped his arms around her.

Burt noticed that Carl was taking the time to cover Doc's body with Doc's own jacket. Burt appreciated that from Carl, Danny didn't need to see something like that, and it got Burt to thinking that he might want to get Danny inside.

"Why don't we move all of this into the house," Burt said. "I think the kitchen should still be relatively intact. And maybe there might be a little of the lobster bisque left." Burt smiled at Lucy, causing her to blush in embarrassment.

The kitchen was still intact. That wasn't too big of a surprise. The kitchen was in another area of the house, after all. Not at all close to where the panic room was located. There was some lobster bisque left, but it had been sitting out in the open for so long that it had made everyone feel like it might be a bit unsafe to eat. So

Burt made peanut butter and jelly sandwiches for everyone as they sat at one of the counters.

"I guess I still don't understand what happened to Doc," Carl said as Burt handed out the sandwiches. "I mean, I understand what was done to him by," Carl looked over at Danny, "well ... his boss. But I just don't get why me doing, well," he looked over and Danny again, "you know, doing what I did helped Doc in any way."

The little girl finished chewing before she spoke, "To go back to our feather pillow analogy, when John Holliday burned through his power, he was left with only that one white feather. That one feather was all that was left of his soul. I was able to fill Doc's pillowcase up by building upon that last feather. Doc then reverted back to the man he was just before he died."

Everyone in the kitchen had forgotten their sandwiches as they took in what the girl was saying. Everyone except Danny who was almost dancing in his seat as he ate.

"Tim, when you and Carl attacked John that last time, he was confused. He didn't know where he was, so he reacted in the only way he knew how. He pulled his guns. We know what happened after that."

They all looked over at Danny.

"What?" Danny asked, his mouth full of food.

They all laughed together.

"Well," the girl continued. "We know what happened after that. Once Carl was," she glanced quickly at Danny, "finished with John, John asked for forgiveness. There's a lot that John had done in his life – his life before his first death – that I'm not happy about. But the one thing John had never done, was to cause the death of a child. In those last few moments, that weighed heavy on his soul, and so he asked for forgiveness. And forgiveness is what he got."

"So Doc is in Heaven?" Carl asked.

"Right where he belongs," the girl replied.

They all finished their sandwiches in silence. The girl then excused herself and rose to leave, but before she could get more than a few steps, Danny jumped down from his seat and ran to her.

"May I hug you?" Danny asked as Burt and Beatrice stood with eyes full of pride.

"Of course, Danny. I would love a hug."

"Thank you," Danny said as he hugged her.

"You are most welcome, Danny."

And with that, she was gone.

Carl left not too long after that, telling Burt that he would be filing a report about the incident with his superiors, but that he would leave out all the stuff about God and the Devil and Doc Holliday's real identity. Doc would just be another John Doe as far as the local police would be concerned.

"Of course," Carl said, tears welling up in his eyes, "there really isn't much left of our police force, or fire department for that matter."

Burt laid a hand on his shoulder.

"They were my friends, Burt. They were good people. God may be able to forgive Doc for killing them all, but I don't know if I ever will."

"I'm sorry, Carl. I really am."

"I'll call the State Police once I'm back at the station. They'll want to know what happened to the troopers they sent here earlier. Of course, I suppose 911 has been lit up like a Christmas tree ever since Doc started firing into that crowd of people outside. I'm sure you'll see some form of law enforcement here before I'm near a phone."

"You can use ours, Carl. It's right there on the wall." Burt pointed at a cordless phone sitting in a cradle on the wall.

"No, that's okay. I think you and Bea and Danny deserve a little quiet before someone shows in an official capacity. It's going to be a while before it's quiet around here again after that happens."

Carl shook Burt's hand, gave Beatrice and Danny a hug, and started to leave.

"Not yet you don't," Lucy shouted to him. She walked over to Carl and hugged him tight before kissing him on the cheek. "Thank you," she said.

"What was that for?" Carl asked as his face went red.

"You saved my life. Doc would have killed me if you hadn't have done what you did. Thank you, Carl."

"Well, I was just doing what any officer of the law would do," Carl said, looking down at his feet in embarrassment.

"You put your life on the line for my girl," Tim said, offering his hand. "You ever need anything, you give me a call."

"I'll do that, thanks."

Burt walked Carl to what used to be the front door and watched as he walked away.

When he got back to the kitchen, Burt saw that Lucy and Tim were preparing to leave.

"So, where are you two off to?" Burt asked once the hugs and handshakes were out of the way.

"The nearest preacher, if she'll have me," Tim said. "What do you say, Lucy?"

"What are you asking me, Tim?" Lucy asked, a little redness creeping up into her cheeks.

Tim dropped to one knee and took her hand in his.

"Will you marry me?"

"Yes! Of course I will!" she cried, tears of happiness and joy streaming down her face.

"I'll tell you what," Burt said. "If you two can wait until everything here calms down, we would love it if the two of you got married right here in our house."

"Oh yes," Beatrice agreed. "We'd love to have the both of you."

"That's a kind offer," Tim said, looking into Lucy's eyes. "But I don't think this can wait. I mean to see the two of us wed as soon as humanly possible."

"I guess that means we're going to Vegas," Lucy smiled.

"Then here," said Burt, reaching into his pocket. He pulled out a set of keys and tossed them to Tim, who caught them deftly.

"What's this?" Tim asked.

"Consider it a wedding present. Those are the keys to my new car."

"What?" Tim asked.

"Well, we can't expect you to walk to Vegas, now can we."

They all laughed and hugged, and soon Tim and Lucy were driving off into the horizon leaving Burt, Beatrice, and Danny alone.

"I guess we got some cleaning up to do," Beatrice said.

"What do say, son?" Burt asked Danny. "You ready to help your mom and dad clean this mess up?"

Burt smiled as he watched Danny give this suggestion some serious thought. Then, after much deliberation, the boy had come to a decision and spoke.

"How about we play Legos instead?"

EPILOGUE

JOHN HENRY "DOC" HOLLIDAY opened his eyes to a blinding white light.

The light dissipated and he found that he sat at a table in a saloon. The white light shone in at him from the street beyond the double swing-back doors. He couldn't make out anything from outside the doors. It was only light, as white as he had ever seen. But the light didn't burn his eyes, as bright as it was. If anything, the light made him feel good and at peace.

Doc took in the saloon. He was alone but for the bartender who stood behind the bar, wiping out glasses with a dirty rag and just generally ignoring his presence. A deck of cards lay on the table in front of him along with a glass of whisky and a lit cigar smoldering away in an ash tray. He wasn't sure what it was about this place, but he felt comfortable here. He felt as if he'd been here before, though he knew he hadn't. It was almost as if parts of the saloon were made up of all his favorite saloons from Ft. Griffith, Dodge City, and Tombstone. He had always felt more at home in a saloon, and this one was the homiest yet.

A part of him wanted to get up and explore these new surroundings, see what there was outside, but a larger part of him decided instead to pick up the deck of cards and give them a real good shuffle. He felt that he should stay put. He somehow knew, from somewhere deep inside himself, that he was here to meet someone. Once they arrived, then he would go with them to the place beyond the doors. Out into the light.

So he shuffled the cards, took a drink of the whisky, a long pull from the cigar, and started to deal the cards out before him for a nice game of solitaire.

Soon he heard the distinctive sound of boots on wood from outside, and he looked up as the doors to the saloon swung open and three men walked in. All three were well dressed in black suits with white shirts and black string ties, black hats, and boots. None of them went heeled. Which suddenly made Doc realize that he too was not armed, though the fact did not alarm him in the slightest. Not only did he feel perfectly safe here, he knew all three of these men. They were old friends.

The youngest of the three approached the table first with a broad smile and his arms open wide. Doc stood and the two embraced, pounding each other on the back in the way that men do.

"It's about time you got here, Doc," the young man said, laughing and pounding away at Doc's back. "Don't know what took you so long, but by God it's good to see you!"

"It's good to see you too, Morgan," Doc said, pulling back from the man and holding him by the shoulders at arm's length.

Doc put his left arm around Morgan and held his right hand out to the older of the three men and said, "Virgil, you're looking well. I see you have the use of both arms now."

The older man, Virgil, took Doc's hand in both of his, "Good Lord, Doc. If anyone looks well it's you." The two smiled.

Virgil and Morgan stood aside as Doc and the third man looked each other over.

"Wyatt," Doc said, inclining his head slightly in a nod of salutations.

"Doc," Wyatt replied, returning the head nod.

"You two girls best stop holding hands and pouring your hearts out all over the place here. You're making the bunch of us uncomfortable," Morgan cajoled.

They all laughed as Doc and Wyatt embraced.

"I missed you, Doc," Wyatt said.

"I missed you too, Wyatt. It's been too long."

They held their embrace for a moment longer before stepping back from each other.

"Well, let's go, Doc," Wyatt said, gesturing to the doors.

"Lead on Wyatt," Doc said, clapping his friend on the back as they made their way to the front of the saloon. "I'm as ready as I ever will be."

And so the four men walked out of the saloon and into the light. Three brothers, and a cherished friend.

The bartender smiled quietly to himself as he watched them go. And suddenly, standing in the place of the bartender was a little girl. She was about five or six years old and wore a pair of faded jeans, scuffed white tennis shoes, and a pink shirt with a big white star in the center of it. Her short, light brown hair was done up in no less than seven pigtails spread out across the top of her head while her bangs rested just above her eyebrows.

"Welcome home, John," she whispered.

The End

AUTHOR'S FINAL THOUGHTS

Here's the part where I thank all the people who helped make this story possible. But before I do, I feel I should explain the thought behind the use of a character that, for some, may have come straight out of left field. I can say, with all honesty, that the inclusion of Doc Holliday into this tale was nothing more than an act of purest whimsy.

Originally, the Beast was going to be the big bad of the tale, but the further I got in to it, the more I began to think that it might be more fun to throw an even bigger bad in there and turn the Beast into one of the good guys and allow him, of course, to get the girl. At the time, I worked nights and weekends as a Photo Specialist for a local pharmacy. I had a notebook with me that I would use to write down my thoughts and ideas for this, and other, stories, and it was as I stood at the end of the massive photo printer, boxing up print after print as they fell out the far end, that the idea of Doc Holliday first took hold.

At first, the big bad that would show up at the Brick House and kill Colin was meant to be a hulking, cigar smoking, red skinned demon with the head of red gorilla and ram's horns. Then I started to think that maybe the villain should be a villain from one of the old fairy tales. The problem was that no one I liked really sprang to mind.

Then Doc Holliday walked into my brain room, sat down, poured himself a drink, and said hello. I was against it at first. It didn't make sense. What does Doc Holliday have to do with Goldilocks and Three Bears, or even fairy tales in general? But then the idea took hold and made me smile as I imagined the possibilities. It really wasn't until I thought of using Doc Holliday that the ending of the story really began to take hold. Up until that point I was literally just making it up as I went, no end in sight, and no idea where I was going. Then came Doc and everything just fell into place.

So, while I *was* worried that readers would throw the book down in disgust (which I wouldn't recommend if you're reading the eBook) when the reveal of the big bad turned out to be Doc Holliday, my own selfishness won out in the end, and I soldiered onward with my folly.

Okay, it's on the the thanks and the gratitude.

First, I want to thank Harold Jennett. He was a huge support mechanism during the two years it took to write this little tale. He put me on the path, he allowed me to bounce ideas off of him, he created the freaking cover, and he pretty much came up with the title. Thanks, Harold. You are a good friend.

Next, Eric White. Like Harold, he's not only a good friend, he helped a lot as I was designing the cover that I didn't end up using for the book. Harold's was just way better than mine. You know, the one thing they don't tell you when you begin your first steps to self-publish a book is that you need a cover. I mean, yeah, it seems pretty obvious, right? But I hadn't really taken it into consideration. I am not an artist. I am not a graphic artist. I am not a man with money who can go out and hire someone to put the cover together for me. And frankly, I had begun to be quite angry that the one thing that was going to stop me from publishing this book, after two years of writing, would be the fact that I couldn't create a cover. Well, I did what I could in Photoshop, but what I had created just didn't look ... professional. That's what Eric did. He stood up and brought that cover to life. Thanks, Eric. Maybe one day I'll use the cover for a variant version or something.

Thanks also to Adam WarRock, MC Frontalot, Mikal kHill, Tribe One, and Kirby Krackle for creating the tunes that kept my mind on the task while I wrote. I can't write without music, and your music is some of the best.

Finally, my family. I have the most loving, most supportive family any man could ever ask for. It's for them that I write. Thank you.

BONUS FEATURES

As I write this, it is July of 2016, five years after I began to write Holliday's Gold.

I was recently looking through an old writing journal of mine, and by writing journal I mean a spiral notebook I bought from a major pharmacy chain. I'd used the journal to write up a scene or two for Holliday's Gold when I was away from a computer, and as I read through it I thought that it might be fun to share with you some of what I found there.

So think of this as the same as the Bonus Features section on a DVD or Blu-ray.

As you read this bonus material, anything in italics will be my thoughts on what I was writing, me thinking it through on paper. I would be writing a scene and then in order to work stuff out in my head, I'd stop and write out what I'd like to do as if I was talking to myself. It's something I still do.

What can I say? It works for me.

I've also tried to capture everything on the page as it was in the journal, including stuff I'd crossed out and then changed.

SEPTEMBER 4, 2011

About the time that ~~Bob Bear learned~~ the Bear family approached the house, and The Beast was being clocked on the head by a wooden rocking chair, a third stranger arrived in town.

Colin was awake, having only been unconscious for a few moments, and was back behind the counter at the Brick House Gas and Groceries, when the electronic bell above the double glass entrance doors sounded, notifying Colin that someone, a customer, had entered the store.

Colin, as per usual, didn't look up from the comic he was reading but instead greeted the customer from the side of his mouth.

"Welcome to Brickhouse Gas and Groceries. Please let me know if I can help you find anything." His voice dripped with mock sincerity.

Colin went back to his comic. He could feel the customer still standing there, just inside the door. The customer's proximity to the sensor was causing the doors to remain open.

Colin groaned inwardly. Hasn't he put up with enough today? The only reason he was even still at work was he was waiting for one of his brothers to relieve him, and he was waiting for the police. ~~After he passed~~ Before the Bear Family left, Beatrice urged Colin to call the police. Actually, she insisted. They wouldn't leave until he did, and until he called one of his brothers.

The customer still hadn't moved.

Colin put on a fake smile, put his comic down, turned towards the customer, and froze in terror. The guy wasn't your typical customer.

He had to have ducked, even turned sideways to get in through the double doors. He stood at least 8 feet tall, and his broad, muscular shoulders were almost as wide.

But that wasn't what was odd about this guy. What was odd was that he was covered in short, red, fur. He looked like a gorilla, but with ram's horns curling on either side of his head. He, or it, wore a black leather vest and baggy black leather pants, but no shoes or boots as his legs ended in hooves.

What was even more frightening where the gun belts that crisscrossed his waist, and the two massive revolvers that hung on each hip.

~~The thing stared at Colin, its right hand resting on the butt of~~ Smoke rolled from the creature's nostrils as it looked at Colin.

"Can I help you?" Colin gulped.

"Why yes, I do believe you can." It spoke like a proper southern gentleman. "I'm looking for my wife. Perhaps you've seen her."

I may need to go back and change up the way this creature looks. I've just had this idea that it might be fun to make this guy Doc Holliday — in demon form. He died all them years ago, and went to Hell. Now he can come to Earth in this form, killing for the Devil.

Maybe. I don't know.

Colin gulps again and stammers out, "Your wife?"

The creature steps up to the counter, looks down on Colin, and smiles. "Yes, my wife. 5-6. 110 pounds. Hair of gold. A regular club girl. Goes by the name of Goldilocks."

Colin's stomach dropped. The Thing smiled, showing large sharp teeth.

"You have seen her. Splendid. Well, my boy. I'm sorry, I didn't catch your name."

"Colin."

"Colin, I'm Doc. It's certainly my pleasure, you can be suer. Here's the thing, Colin. I'm going to make this relatively simple for me. Tell me where she went, and I won't have to do some very, very nasty things to you. They will be quite unpleasant, I can assure. Just point. Point out the direction, and I'll be on my way.

The more I think about this, the more I think it might be fun to keep this guy as Doc Holliday, but not all monstrous and demon-like. He should just look like Doc Holliday. He's skinny, and frail, and has some sort of powers. Colin can sense it, that's why he's so scared.

Colin, speechless, pointed a shaky finger in the direction that Goldilocks went.

Or maybe, because Doc is so frail and skinny, maybe Colin isn't afraid of him. Of course, the guy is packing heat, and after Colin's day, I think he will be scared. Regardless, I don't this Colin will survive. OK, so Colin points . . .

"Thank you, son. You've done me a great service today."

SEPTEMBER 6, 2011

I want to write a new intro for Goldilocks. Possibly with Goldilocks herself fleeing from DOC. But I have to do it in such a way that ~~we don't~~ I don't name her as Goldilocks. I think the scene I have now which introduces her is pretty good, but maybe I can take some from what I have now and use it in the new intro.

Her name was Lucy, though no one called her that anymore. She was 27 and alone. But alone was what she wanted.

SEPTEMBER 17, 2011

There are a few things that need to be done to complete the Goldilocks story.

Goldilocks tells the bears that the man in black is Doc Holliday and that he is her husband. The Beast over hears and is not happy. "Your husband!"

Doc Holliday's story. Why is he now really, really evil — and still alive.

The fight. Doc vs. The Beast, and Officer Carl Friendly — Doc is destroyed.

Goldilocks (Lucy) and The Beast (Tim) live happily ever after?

Goldilocks ran. She had no idea where she was going, she just knew that she had to get as far away as possible. She could hear the Bears following her, yelling her name, telling her to stop, but she wouldn't listen, won't listen. They didn't understand. No one understood. No one but her and Doc. And the Devil too, she supposed.

She ran through the house like a woman possessed, which was how Goldilocks felt. Possessed with absolute terror. The turned this way and that, taking pathways at random.

Goldilocks suddenly found herself at the end of a long hallway which ended in a large door. The door had no handle. Only a key pad.

Fear is a great motivator, second only to pain. But you get both pain and fear together, there isn't much in this life you can't accomplish.

However, this isn't infallible. Goldilocks is proof of that. She spent years under the thumb of her husband, ~~yet in the end, she left. Because when it comes right down to it, everyone has a line. A line that once crossed is the~~ suffering from his torture, both physical and emotional. Living with the fear he laid upon her.

SEPTEMBER 18, 2011

Fear is a great motivator, second only to pain. And when you introduce fear to pain, there isn't much you can't get someone to do.

But there are limits, it's not an infallible motivational tool. Goldilocks is proof of that. Everyone has a line. Everyone has a point, that when pushed over that line, that person (I was apparently done writing that day as it just ends).

OCTOBER 9, 2011

Tim, The Beast, came to amidst smoke and ruin. One moment the kid was screaming, the next, they were falling. Then all went black.

All in all, Tim was getting rather tired of passing out. He figured that he might want to see a doctor at some point. Passing out as many times as he had in the last twenty-four hour period ~~can't~~ couldn't be good for one's physical health or mental well being.

Tim stood and brushed himself off. It was difficult staying on his feet, which had nothing to do with his multiple blackouts. No, it was hard to stay balanced due to the fact that the floor was pitched at a near ~~forty-five~~ fifteen degree angle.

Tim looked around. He saw a big clump of brown fur that he guessed was the three bears, but he didn't see Goldilocks anywhere.

"Goldilocks," Tim called out, the dust in the air making him cough.

Tim noticed a large hole in the wall. The steel looked like it had been completely melted through. But what could do that?

"Goldilocks," he called again, stumbling around the room. "Where are you, baby?"

The Bears began to stir. Bob was the first to his feet, but the other two were quick to follow.

"Goldilocks," Tim yelled.

JANUARY 8, 2012

He had died. He knew that now. In some part of his, brain? Did he even have a brain? He understood that he was dead. But how was he capable of understanding? Of thinking?

He was dying. He understood that. He'd come to accept it. ~~He lay in the bed that had been his home for the past few months. The bed resided in the institution in Glenwood Springs, Colorado.~~

~~He was dying and he knew that it wouldn't be much longer.~~

Prelude opens with Doc, dying in his bed in Glenwood Springs, CO. Sun is shinning. His name is not mentioned, the year is not mentioned. There are clues to his identity. He is dying of TB. He was once a dentist. He was a gambler and a killer. The nurse, or sister (I will have to look that up) comes in. He doesn't want her to see that he is crying as he thinks of all the bad he's done. He yells at her, cursing and spitting. She flees.

As he lay in the bed that had been his home for these many months, he thought back over his life. ~~He had regrets.~~ He had made some though choices in his day. Abandoning his dental practive. Mixing with the wrong people. The lives he'd taken through violence. He had killed a great many men. Ended their lives with as little effort as it took to fall out of a chair.

Killing had always come easy to him. Killing, and gambling, and carousing. That's what had become of his life. And here is where it brought him. Laid up and dying in Glenwood Springs, Colorado.

A nurse came into the room with a pitcher of water. She made the typical clinical fuss about him.

He closeded his eyes before the tears came. He yelled and used words to browbeat the nurse from the room. Words were all he had left. They, now, were his only weapon. A weapon he used quite often. Besides, it would not do for the woman to see his tears. Not from him. His name was known and could still strike fear in the hearts of men.

So he yelled. He spit and he cursed until the nurse ran from the room. His yells turned to coughs. And uncontrollable coughing that bent him double, that sent pain throughout his body, and flecked his lips with blood.

This was his price. The price he paid for the life he led and the live he ended. Everything had a price. His price was this bed.

His yelling causes a coughing fit and blacks out.

When he comes to, the room is dark. Doc is not alone. He feels someone else in the room. He calls out.

A light appears. A man, the most beautiful man Doc had ever seen, is standing in the light.

The man tells Doc that he is dead and that it is time for him to pass on to another place.

Doc asks the man if he is God. The man says he has been called such before.

Doc tries to ask for forgiveness. The man stops him. He tells Doc that HE forgives him. There is no need ask.

He asks Doc if he wants to come with him and Doc agrees.

JANUARY 12, 2012

Just a couple of quick Goldilocks ideas:

In the prelude, Doc is angry that he is dying. He's not made piece with it.

The nuns at the institution in Glenwood Springs try to get him to ask for forgiveness, but he refuses. He lived his life the only way he knew how. He's not even sure he believes in God. Why he be dying the way he was if there was a loving God looking over him.

A man visits Doc. A man in a suit and bowler hat with a large bushy mustache. He tells Doc to call him Boss. He tells Doc that he can help him. He can cure him of his illness. He can take him somewhere to make him better. Doc agrees.

I like the idea of Doc having to sign a contract. But I'm not sure yet. I see the Boss holding out a parchment for Doc to sign, Doc doesn't have anything to sign it with, the Boss has him hold open his hand. The Boss runs his index finger along the palm of Doc's hand, making an X. The X splits open and Doc's hand fills with blood. *A few drops drip onto the parchment, the Boss says that their pact is sealed, everything goes white.*

JULY 2, 2013

I have finished my second draft if Goldilocks. For the time being I am calling it The Bears, the Beast, and the Blonde. It came in at a little over 46,500 words.

I feel like I should add more about Carl Friendly, and possibly more to the final battle, but I'll wait until a few folks I've given it to read it and I get their opinions.

JULY 20, 2013

Just when I thought I was done with Goldilocks, I've reached the conclusion that I may need to do some big changes simply because of Doc Holliday. I'm beginning to realize that Doc just doesn't match up. So I have three choices.

Ignore it and change nothing.

Change Doc Holliday to the Big Bad Wolf. That means I would have to rewrite the prologue and epilogue, which I don't really want to do. However, the idea of the Beast fighting the Big Bad Wolf is appealing.

Make Goldilocks, the three bears, and Colin, humans based on the fairy tale characters. I this more appealing than #2, but it does change what I wanted to do with this book.

I'm going to go go forward here to come up with ideas if I stay with Doc Holliday.

The Griswolds will become the Behrs, or frankly, they can stay the Griswolds as it sounds somewhat like grizzly.

Carl Friendly can be a decendant of Wyatt Earp, and I do think I should use more of him.

What I may do is work up a new version of the story. Goldilocks will be Lucy who's club name is Goldilocks.

HERE ENDS THE BONUS MATERIALS

ABOUT THE AUTHOR

Steeven R. Orr lives as a recluse with his wife and three children somewhere in the hills of Eastern Kansas. When he's not helping with homework, or running errands, or paying bills, or working, or spending time with his family, or sleeping, or eating, or using the bathroom, Steeven likes to write.

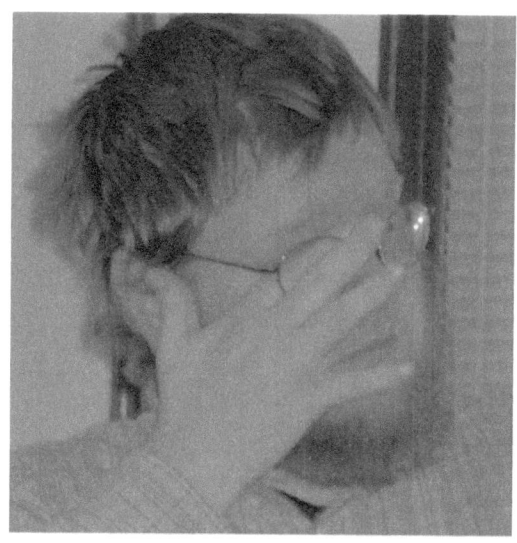

CONTACT

WWW.STEEVENORRELSE.COM

BOOKS@STEEVENORRELSE.COM